Sturgis Winters
and the
Money Tree
Part One

by d. Levine©

The Wisdom of Silence

Introduction
Visitors from near and far are enjoying the last few warm days before
the season change. Fishermen are busy securing boats. Folding, packing
their colorful dry fishing nets for the long cold winter ahead. Most birds
have flown south. Just a few locals remain trying to get that last fill
before the long flight out. Soon Mr. Strouss' pumpkin patch will be
filled with big shiny ripe pumpkins. What he calls his "shiny delicious
beauties" as they make their way down the green grassy bluff to market
or roadside sale. The hunter's ax will be hard at work chopping wood to
warm homes and firesides. Children tightly bundled up with runny red
noses will have fun playing, laughing, skating on streams, lakes or ponds
frozen solid again this year.

Out back at the gift shop beyond the rope swing, that old wooden barn,
badly in need of repair, with the rusted wagon wheel lying against it,
will remain in place again this year, no time for repairs. Shortly, winter
will display her virgin snow of the season. And beautiful fresh cut, pine
trees, pine cones and bright red poinsettia, will be for sale at every
corner, helping to invite the holiday fragrance into homes. Rushing
holiday shoppers will line the snow slushed roads in horse driven
carriages. Many will be headed to Nan's Gift Shop for Buy, Sale or
Trade… And it seems that everyone who enters the door of Nan's Gift
Shop has an interesting life experience story to share…

Nan, Alex and Asza are out making their morning treasure hunt along
the beach, looking for washed ashore items from the ocean the night
before. Most items in Nan's Gift Shop have come from the sea. Alex
hitched the horse to the wagon and made a nice soft pallet for E-la the
cat to lay on for their long ride. Having just finished eating, feeling a
little lazy, she stretched, licked her paws, wiped her face and decided to
wait on the porch for their return. Knowing if she went or stayed, it
didn't matter. Nan would bring back a chunky fresh piece of tuna, her
favorite fish, for her to enjoy.

"This will be the last early morning hunt for the season. The weather has
started to change. It's getting too cold and foggy. Soon the fog will be
too thick, obscuring our view," Nan said walking alongside the sun-
bleached wagon looking for finds. As the wagon moved slowly its
wheels squeaking from many trips of picking up soft, moist sand along
the beach, gave way to the music they needed to sing their treasure hunt
song. As its wheels turned leaving in the sand one of many indentations
of oversized screws needed to hold the rear wheels intact, making this
possibly its last journey before being replaced with a new. Alex led in
singing their song… "Treasure hunting is fun. What we find. We keep,
give to no one. Unless askers are pirate ghosts then we gladly give them
gold before they cut our throats," he laughed, repeated. "Whoa," Nan

said pulling back on the horses' reins, bringing the wagon to a complete stop. "You know Alex it's been a while since we found something. Hmmm, let me see. Hey! I know a spot not many people know about. But it's on a remote part of the beach near Cliff Rocks. Let's go over there, Alex we're sure to find something there," Alex was a little tired but he was still anxious in his reply, "That will be fine Nan I'm ready. Let's go!"

As they road awhile Alex looked ahead glancing at the shoreline for any unclaimed sea cargo. That may have washed ashore the night before. They finally reached the remote area. Then right away Nan spotted several loose crates, wooden barrels and leather strapped chests that were pushed to the shore when the tide came in still floating at the water's edge. "Oh! Look Alex, boxes, crates, and other stuff!" Nan was so excited she dropped the horses' reins from her hands. She started running toward her find.

"Oh! My goodness… This is a big find!" Nan said. Even Asza the bird agreed with the excitement he flew around in circles flapping, fluttering his wings while chattering, often embellishing the truth at the same time losing his feathers in the air from the excitement of Nan's find. "Look what I found! This is a big find I told you guys to come here," Asza squawked. Nan was right. The find was huge. Alex too was smiling as he reached underneath the wagon front seat for Nan's incoming merchandise ledger book to list items found on today. On the sheets of paper, he listed several wooden leather strapped chests containing vintage wine, rare cognac, untouched dry spices, lead crystal stemware, Egyptian linen, sets of royal silverware and unopened jewelry boxes, probably from a shipwreck of long ago. With all the excitement and commotion over Nan's new discovery, there was a box that was almost overlooked. Still floating near the water's edge, one box that floated alone, it was thickly encased in layers of candle wax with the wordage "Throw Back into the Sea" Nan picked it up, read the words out loud, looked at Alex and said, "Well…what do you think I should do. Shall I do what it says?" Alex was slow to answer. He then took the box from Nan looked at the words written on it and said, "Yes ma'am. We have enough stuff already. A great find here, see! Go ahead Nan…throw it back into the sea. I would if I were you." He said handing Nan back the box. Still frantically flying around in circles, chattering Asza the bird mimicked Alex… "Go ahead throw it back into the sea. Throw it back into the sea I would if I were you." Nan stood looking at the box for a while holding it in her hands. Then she held the box firmly in her left hand, drew it all the way back, stopping in mid motion, almost giving in to their cries of concerns, She lowered the box, looking at it closely, shaking it. Putting the box up to her ear listening for sounds of a broken container inside, Nan lowered it, looking at the box again, reasoning with herself. *"If I throw it back into the sea, something of value like diamonds, gold, rubies or maybe even both might be inside. And someone else would get them. Hmmm...I don' know what to do,"* she *sighed.* Nan stood by the wagon pondering on what she should do with the box. Then she turned looked at Alex and said, "I'll tell you what Alex. I'll take it back to the shop, open it, see what's inside, and if nothing's valuable inside then I will toss it back into the sea," she concluded. With apprehension Alex said, "Oh... No! Ma'am I don't know about that idea, ma'am. I'd just throw it back like Asza said. Besides we have more than enough stuff here already. See! Look Nan!" Alex wanted Nan not to take the box, but heed the warning written on it. He wanted her to be content with items they actually had. "See Nan...see for yourself. "He said trying to convince her as he loaded the wet sandy cargo in back of the wagon from the day's hunt. Nan stood smiling looking at the cargo find for the day and said. "Well, Alex, maybe you're right. Maybe what you said made a lot of sense. But shush, my mind is made up. I'm taking the box with me." "But Nan we," he tried to replied before being cut off by Nan "Shush...Alex. It's not going to do you any good to discuss this matter any further, my mind is made up this conversation is closed," "Yeah, my mind is made up," squawked the bird. Alex realized his discussion with Nan regarding the box was unsuccessful so he finished the light inventory; they loaded the rest of their goods, ate lunch, and rested a while.

Soon after resting Nan decided to call it a day with half a wagon filled it was already pointed south in the direction of home. But before leaving, she and Alex looked around checking to make sure no items were left behind. As they looked around she noticed something bright yellow floating out in the ocean due north near Cliff Rocks. "What might that be out there?" she asked. "Out where?" Alex replied. "There! You guys see that, don't you?" she said. "See what?" Alex said. "Out there, see it! That, bright yellow stuff moving in the waters near those rocks don't you see that?" Nan said pointing toward its direction, "Where?" Alex replied, putting his hand up near his face to block out the sun to take a closer look. "Ooh! That yellow stuff. Yeah! Yes, Nan. Now I see it!" he commented, "What could it be Alex?" she asked him. "I don't know Nan, what do you think it is?" he asked her. "I don't know either Alex. I can't tell," she replied. Nan looked down at her wrist watch checking the time. "Well...honestly I can't tell from here but there's only one sure way to find out now isn't there," she said turning the horse around heading closer to Cliff Rocks before the sun set. The ride wasn't that long, but still, no one felt like singing anymore treasure hunt songs. And Asza their echo singer was already asleep, perched on top of the wagon seat railing. As they rode closer to their destination neither one could figure out what was moving out there in the water. They could see the yellow stuff which turned out to be yellow fishing net indicator flags. But beyond that there was still something else out there in the waters bobbing, moving, badly entangled in those big rocks. From a distance, it looked to be an animal of some sort. But as the wagon moved in closer, they could clearly see and what Nan saw was more than she could stomach, she gasped almost fainting.

It was a woman, badly, beaten and bruised, with a gash to the back of her head. Her lower body was snarled in fishing net, with hooks stuck in her flesh. Alex and Nan both were stunned, sadden and at a loss for words. In Nan's attempt to help the injured woman she jumped from the slow-moving wagon rushed over to assist the hurt woman who was pinned to the rocks. They could see her but getting to her wouldn't be that easy. Alex heard Nan whisper, "Oh! No! No! No! This can't be happening," Grabbing her stomach to prevent from vomiting but to no avail Nan vomited then screamed for help. "Help someone!" "Help anyone! Help! Help! Help!" they both shouted and yelled. Nan said. "Alex, go back to the wagon! Go!" she pleaded. "Is she dead?" Alex asked, before leaving. "I don't know, Alex. It's hard to tell. As you can see she's stuck to those rocks out there. She caught, tangled in fishing net and these big waves won't let me get to her," Nan told Alex "I think I can cut her loose. I have a knife in my pocket. If only I can reach her! Hurry, Alex. Throw me a stick. There's one in the wagon, hurry! Help somebody! Help me," Alex shouted. Nan started to really think she couldn't rescue that woman all by herself. It was too dangerous. So she dropped the knife and stick on the sandy beach. And yelled looking around for help…waiting for someone to come, but no one came. Nan knew then it was a matter of life or death she had to find enough courage within herself to step out onto the sharp jagged rocks. To cut free the woman without hooking herself too badly or being knocked down by those strong, cold, waves. So Nan picked back up the knife and the stick she waited a few seconds to mustering up enough courage then Nan stepped out on the sharp rocks, wobbling, trying to keep her balance from falling. She fought the cold currents tugging on the fishing net, pulling on the net, cutting it and hooking herself again, Nan lost her balance and slipped into the sea.

Getting back up, she yanked, cut and pulled, drenched, shivering from the icy cold, waters slipping, losing her balance again, falling into the sea. Nan climbed back onto the big rocks refusing to give up. And on the third attempt she finally found her footing. She yanked on the fishing nets, slipped, but caught her balance; cutting the net finally freeing the woman. Nan was happy, relieved, exhausted breathing hard between words trying to catch her breath while speaking to Alex at the same time. "I think she's alive, Alex! I think she's alive…but just barely," Nan checked the woman's wrist for a pulse, talking to her looking at her, then Nan slowly drew back her hand, removing it entirely off the wrist of the survivor looking confused. "Oh, Alex, wait," she started off slowly saying…" She alive Alex but It's not a woman. It's a man! It's a man!" she shouted to Alex who was standing on the shore. Seconds later he shouted back, "A man are you sure, Nan?" "Yes, Alex it's a man!" Nan yelled back. And with everything going on she or Alex didn't have time to notice but was glad to see a group of last minute beach goers that heard their screams for help. They wrapped the wounded man in their beach towels and blankets, helping Nan load him into the back of her wagon. They also gave her a blanket to keep herself warm until she got back to the shop to change her wet clothing. They thanked the beachgoers. Then Nan told Alex as she carefully raced the wagon back into town, "As soon as we get closer in, run, hurry, don't stop for anything. Get Dr. Laris and get his quick. This man's life depends on it!" "Yes ma'am, you can count on me," Alex quickly replied.

When the doctor arrived, Hilda, Nan and Alex had already made room for the injured stranger. They laid him in Nan's bed. He was still unconscious's. Dr. Laris rushed into the shop then into Nan's room leaving the door opened. They heard him say "What the hell?" He called Nan and Hilda into the room trying to find out what happened to this man by asking more questions, "Who is he? Who could do such a terrible inhumane act to another human being?" Nan told the doctor they didn't know anything about this man. "That's sad," he replied, disappointed with their answer. He was hoping one of them would know something, anything about the badly injured man. He wanted to make more inquiries but, he needed to focus his attention back on the bruised, beaten, hooked man. Dr. Laris hurried them out of the room closing the door. The doctor gently examined the stranger, trying not to inflect any more unnecessary pain on the patient. But then, right in the middle of his examination, Dr. Laris stopped, stared at the face of the man, slightly smiling. He continued the examination and upon completion the doctor came out of the room, telling them the stranger was fortunate to be alive. That he had no broken bones, some water in his lungs and a few bruises. "He took a bad blow to the head. Also, having deep cuts from the fish hooks I gave him something for pain. I think he'll pull through this. He's still young and strong. But it's a good thing he's unconscious. In the meantime, we will have to pull those hooks out, right away before anymore infection sets in. I will need plenty of hot water, soap and clean white towels. Oh! When the nurse comes send her right in will you please?" "Yes, doctor," Hilda answered. "And keep the hot coffee coming" he expressed, rolling up his long sleeves to wash his hands "…and if you got any good brandy, I can use some of that too for myself." Then Dr. Laris hurried went back into the room to start medical treatment on the sick man.

The waiting seemed like an eternity. All through the house groans were heard. Then a moment of silence, followed by the sound of metal fishing hooks dropping onto a bent silver tray Nan had given the nurse to help assist the doctor with removal of infected hooks endured by the stranger. Hours passed. Finally, it was all over Dr. Laris came out of the room. He informed them of the medical care he had administered to the patient. "I removed all fish hooks, applied medicated gauze with several layers of thick bandages to the infected areas. By the way do any of you know someone named Josie?" Dr. Laris asked standing in the bedroom doorway, removing his eye glasses to clean them. "The stranger kept muttering that name or I think that's what he was trying to say. I couldn't make his words out to clear," He told them. Then Nan, Alex and Hilda looked at each other waiting for one of them to answer "yes or no" to the doctor's question. But no one did. Each told him they had never seen the stranger before, just as they had told him earlier, when he asked. Well then let me put it to you this way. "Have any of you heard the name Josie mentioned around here, before?" He continued asking. And the answer was the same. "No!" "Well in that case let's put a temporary closure to this sad saga for now. It is my opinion it is safe to say the stranger's injured body must have come from up river somewhere near Mermaid's Bay and washed down with the tide but that's just my theory. Anyway, he's a very sick man keep him quiet, warm and still. We don't want him to go into shock and make sure you give him his medicine on time. I will be back later to check on him. But as for now all we can do is wait," he told them. "Yes, doctor, I agree with you. That poor soul lying in there, all we can do now is wait," Hilda sadly expressed, as she walked into the next room with the nurse to see if she could be of any help. Later, Dr. Lairs pulled Nan to the side he whispered. "You know Nan... I've delivered lots of babies in my time boy babies and girl babies. I even delivered you. I've seen the boys grow into manhood. But in all my years of practice I have never seen a man that good looking before," He shared with her trying to keep his voice low. Then Dr. Laris took in a deep breath almost repeating his words. "Nope, have not, never in all my years of practice, strange, isn't it? Oh well? And Nan don't take what I'm about to say next the wrong way but there's something about that man in the room, the patient. I mean. I can't pin point it right now, but there's something about him," he told her, scratching his head then pushing back the glasses from off the tip of his nose back onto his face. As he reached for his coat to leave Nan assisted him with his coat then she replied. "Well...It may be something to what you just, said Doc. I'll keep that in mind" she said smiling," "Please do, Nan," he was serious in his reply looking her straight into the eyes, not smiling. "Oh! Nan before I forget here's something for those fish hook shags you have on your hands. This medicine should quickly help heal them," the doctor said taking in a deep breath then exhaling. "I've been extremely busy today. I was on my way up to Mr. Kingsly when I got your message from Alex about the stranger. Nan, you know Mr. Kingsly is excited today, his mare is about to foal," "Is she really?" Nan said almost laughing with joy for him. "Yeah, he's pretty ecstatic, right about now. "I bet he is," she replied. "And I'll tell him you send your best regards," "Would you please Doc Laris and thank you for coming," she said. As the doc was about to leave he stopped again at the door and said "I know. I said I was leaving those other times. I know. I've been here much too long already but I must tell you this before I leave...It's a good thing you found that man, when you did, before the cold front rolled in. I can tell you this, Nan. He would not have survived those icy waters too much longer before anyone or if anyone would have discovered him in time. Oh and daaaa, one more thing the nurse or I will come to change bandages on the patient's lower torso," Doc said, watching Nan blush. Send for me if you need me. But for now, I gotta go," he said leaving the shop in a hurry.

Nan temporarily closed the gift shop. Rumors began to spread, all of them started by Mrs. Utley, the banker's wife, but Nan didn't care she was busy taking care of her unexpected houseguest, Nan was devoted to him giving the stranger all the care, compassion and attention he needed to have a successful recovery. She wanted to make sure she was the one who nursed him back to good health. Nan sat by his bedside talking to him during the day. Then she would softly sing to him at night waiting for him to wake up out of his unconsciousness. Eventually, he did.

It was on a cold, early Tuesday morning when he woke up. Shouting! Screaming! Putting his hands over his eyes! "My eyes, my eyes I can't see! What happened to my eyes?" Nan did her best to calm him down by telling him to please lie still. "You have been in an accident but you are safe now. The doctor is on his way to see about you." Her soft voice along with her gentle touch calmed him down, eased his fears. He was able to relax and later asked. "Where am I? What happened to me?" Nan told him to please remain still. "Hilda, keep an eye out for his carriage," she said. "Right Nan," Hilda yelled watching from the shop window for the doctor's carriage to pull up. Hilda thought it would be a good idea to make a fresh hot kettle of tea just in case the doctor or someone else would want a cup. She put the kettle on then went into the gift shop. "It's here Nan! His carriage is here, ma'am," Hilda shouted running back to the kitchen from the gift shop window. When Dr. Laris came through the door, Hilda offered him a hot cup of tea he accepted it after examining the stranger. His visit was brief telling Nan the stranger was doing well, that he should be just fine and that his healing is in the normal range. The doctor also told her, he removed the medical apparatus from the patient's right arm. He told her that she, Hilda along with Alex did a great job with the stranger's recovery and they save that man's life. "You should all be proud of yourselves," Dr. Laris said, further saying that the stranger's blindness with his memory loss was probably from a blow to the head. They both should return as his body heals. Nan was so glad. She stood facing Dr. Laris smiling, excited asking him "When? When will they return?" Nan asked. "I don't know for sure his memory along with his sight could come back tomorrow or it could take seven months or longer. Depending on the severity of the injury and how quickly the patient heals." he added. The doctor told Nan to continue giving the patient his medicines. Then Dr. Laris reached into his medical bag he pulled out a small brown glass bottle of eye drops. "For your patient," he said smiling. "Give as directed." He continued to inform her, the injured man will need a cane as soon as his legs are strong. He will also have to wear dark glasses to protect his eyes, until his sight returns. "About seven months the doctor said," she happily thought. Nan needed to hear those words. They were comforting to her. "Seven months or longer" she whispered, with a smile on her face. "Or shorter," The doc shouted back at her smiling walking out the door to his carriage.

Nan was 44 years old she had always been alone. She never had a man in her life or even been kissed. Her whole life had been centered-around the gift shop and the people in the town in which she lived.

She had friends that grew up with her, but no one would ever seriously consider dating or marrying her. Nan had gotten used to being along. She always felt empty, incomplete, inside isolated. And having to live with that constant reminder of being rejected by men only made her feel part of a woman. But, now! With the stranger in her life, maybe now she will know what it means to be needed by a man or to feel the full experience of feeling like a whole woman even if it's just temporary.

The sign in the gift shop window told briefly why the shop was closed. Customers that came by read it and understood. Others like Mrs. Utley simply would not take no for an answer. Hilda could see her getting out of Mrs. Utley's black enamel carriage with gold trim around the doors. She was waiting for her to get to the door. As she approached the shop door Mrs. Utley rang the doorbell. She was greeted by Hilda then asked in her high-pitched voice, "Well good day Hilda, is the proprietor of this establishment in?" she asked. "She is," Hilda was quick to answer she was blocking the door so Mrs. Utley could not look into or enter the shop. "Now tell me Hilda, how long is the shop going to be closed and where is, that Nan Sumpter?" she rudely inquired. Hilda went on to ask her whether or not she had read the sign, and if she had she would know that Nan was busy taking care of a very sick man. "A very sick man, ha, my eye! I bet she is. Now, come on you can do better than that, one. We've all heard around here the not so nice things that might be going on in there. And Hilda you know I'm not the one to carry a bone but I must drop this one on your plate. Nan is an unmarried woman and it's my understanding that she's touching on a naked man in there. Or playing nurse is what they say she's calling it. Doesn't that girl realize she has a reputation to uphold? And tell her for me she's losing a lot of money along with loyal customers, like myself if I may add, that can't wait forever, for her to stop playing doctor. You can also tell her for me that she needs to reopen this gift shop right now! Immediately! Today! I insist!" Mrs. Utley shouted, stomping her left foot, breaking the high-heel on her shoe, saying, "Oh, look Hilda! Look what you've gone and made me do. It's all, your fault! Yes, it is. If the shop had been opened none of this would ever had happened. Oh, just look and these were my favorite pair of Peau de Soie heels, not to mention the most expensive pair in my wardrobe," Mrs. Utley bragged, taking the broken heel, holding it in her hand showing it to Hilda. Hilda had no comment. "And speaking of disappointment, why don't you do something about these street beggars hanging around here. Hey you! Get away from my carriage! Don't put your finger print smudges on it either. No, I don't have any spare change to waste or throw away. Why don't you go out, get an honest job like everyone else or create one for yourself that doesn't require begging," she shouted that to one asker from the gift shop walkway. As she continued to complain, telling Hilda that her driver almost hit one sitting in the middle of the road on the way over and if he had, he would not have been responsible.

Mrs. Utley wanted to know if Nan was going to have the shop open in time for the Governor's Ball. "I can't honestly say," Hilda replied. "Well, then tell her again for me it would be a shame if she missed another Governor's Ball again this year. Along with losing valuable customers," Mrs. Utley stated pointing to herself. "Not to mention the revenue we contribute to this gift shop. My! My! And to lose it all behind a fantasy would be shameful. Wouldn't you think, Hilda?" laughing she said, at the same time trying to look over and around Hilda to get a glimpse into the shop at the stranger. But stout Hilda was blocking her at every movement. Finally, Mrs. Utley soon came to realize she was defeated in not succeeding with her intimidating verbiage at Hilda, she grew tired leaving frustrated, hobbling away down the walkway mumbling under her breath, "My stars the extremes a woman will go through just to get a man playing rescue nurse in there. And I'm supposed to believe that tall tale. Preposterous, ha! Don't make me laugh!" Hilda watched with pity and pleasure in her heart for Mrs. Utley as she limped away. Thinking to herself it would take an epiphany to change that woman's behavior and Hilda doesn't have that kind of power. With Mrs. Utley leaving Hilda took a few steps outside to straighten the gift shop sign in front. She felt sorry for Mrs. Utley's, but she was also glad that Mrs. Utley was finally leaving. And just as Mrs. Utley was about to step into her black shiny carriage, from out of nowhere, Fob the beggar, appeared standing there silent with grey piercing eyes, a long thin face, wearing a green crooked soiled hat with a fox insignia on the brim. Grinning at her, he asked, "Some change for a cold hungry man?" Mrs. Utley looked at Fob in disgusted then she rolled her eyes at him, "Out of my way!" she said, using her broken high heel along with one of her black leather elbow gloves to shoo him away. But he didn't move. He was looking at Mrs. Utley's new carriage, smiling, knowing carriages are expensive and she must have a lot of money. He was blocking the door to her carriage preventing her from getting in. She stood looking at Fob in the face and said. "Do you know who I am?" Fob taking some time to answer finally said, "No! Why'd you ask? Should I?" "How dare you talk to me in that manner, you fool! Out of my way, you true simpleton," she shouted. Fob not moving an inch said, "Well, then let me change things up a bit. Give me some money. I know you got it. I see your new carriage and I'm hungry," "You impossible idiot! Something must be wrong with you! Move…Get out of my way! You, total nincompoop," she being upset, shouted. But Mrs. Utley wasn't really upset because of Fob. She was really upset because Nan's gift shop was still closed. And she couldn't get any information from Hilda to gossip to others about and the fact that she had broken the heel on her favorite pair of shoes didn't help her situation either. Mrs. Utley was truly disappointed. So she humored herself by emulating Fob's words in a voice like his *"change for a hungry man,"* "Well, you're right on one thing! You're skinny enough to be hungry, but a man you are not!" To that Fob laughed. Then replied, "Well the first part's true but I can prove the second," Mrs. Utley sharply replied, "Why...you snake! "Aup! Wait! Wait a minute! Hold it! I've seen you before. Why...You're that thief. You stole my husband's wallet!" She shouted pointing at him, then he quickly replied, "Who me?" Fob innocently smiling said. "Yes you! It was you! You stole his wallet! You slimy pick-picketer," she yelled. Upon hearing those words Fob moved out of her way letting Ms. Utley board. He went on to tell Mrs. Utley that he wears many hats in life but wouldn't confess to wearing that one. "Proof my good woman. You need proof...until then stop slandering my good name," He said, looking at Mrs. Utley in-that-kind-of-way, smiling. She gasped, "Why, you insinuating fool. How dare you even suggest! Get away from my carriage and how dare you breathe the same air as me? Driver! Driver! Take me home immediately!" she yelled. "Yes, Mrs. Utley right away," The fearful driver replied moving slow as his hands shook grabbing on to the horses reins. Fob stood next to Mrs. Utley's carriage as it rode off. He removed his dirty green hat he held in his hand laughing. Straightening his soiled clothing to look presentable. Fob then bowed from the waist down saying to her carriage as it departed, "Madam, I bid you a fond farewell, a fond farewell." He laughed even louder as her carriage drove off further down the road, soon after he meandered to several other shops, standing outside, begging for money but being refused by women that passed his way. Fob decided to approach a well-dressed man who gave in to his asking, giving him enough money to buy a hot meal for the night. The man left Fob in the restaurant eating then he decided to stop eating and start asking customers for money. He was also caught swiping tips from off tables inside the restaurant. Fob was then quickly told to leave never to return again.

Months passed before Fob's begging led him to an elite residential cove. He knocked on doors asking for money, frightening some residents. Ringing doorbells, using his long fingernail to frighten, scare intimidate residents living in the area, "The house with the big Christmas holly wreath on the door will be next," he thought to himself. A maid came to the door answering his ring. "Yes, sir, may I help you?" she asked. Fob went on to ask for money, as he had done at the other houses in the cove. Frightened she reached into her apron pocket giving him her money. "Is that all you got?" he rudely said. She told him to wait right there, she would try to find some more. Instead, she went to get the owner of the house. As he came down stairs he saw Fob at the door. "Well...I hear you want money. Are you willing to work for it?" he asked. "Why…yesss that is correct and Yes, I am." But what Fob didn't realize is that the house he was standing in was the home and doorway of Mrs. Utley. And he was talking to Mr. Utley. Fob went on to say he was laying down his working guidelines before he'd work for any man. He would need for him to sign a gentlemen's agreement. "Ah! A gentlemen's agreement I see," Mr. Utley said stroking his beard. "Now…what might that entail?" Mr. Utley asked. Then he listened to Fob watching his ego swell. He told Mr. Utley all the things he would and would not do on a job, leaning back on heels then forward to his toes, using his hands to help express his conversation, trying to make a good impression. But Mr. Utley kept looking at that one long fingernail on Fob's hand, getting angry but hiding it well. While remembering what his wife told him. Months earlier Mrs. Utley had told her husband about Fob the beggar, what he looked like. What he was wearing at the time of his insults to her, and his grinning at her with his raggedy chipped top front tooth. She described Fob to her husband all the way down to the missing middle finger on his left hand. She even told him about the dirty green crooked felt hat with a fox insignia on the brim. Mrs. Utley went on to tell her husband the way Fob insulted her by making lewd sexual gestures using his body, his tongue with that long fingernail in a lascivious way. And that his rude obnoxious behavior was intolerable and unacceptable. Ironically, Fob was wearing the same clothing as she described when he rang Mr. Utley's doorbell. Mr. Utley never introduced himself. He just told Fob to go around to the back of the house and he would meet him there. And he did. By starting the conversation off with, "So you want money, is that right?" Mr. Utley asked. "Mmmm hmmm," Fob replied. "And are you still willing to work for it?" Mr. Utley asked again, to make sure. "And that is correct again." Fob sarcastically answered. "I see," Mr. Utley expressed. Fob further explained his payment arrangement agreement, telling Mr. Utley this agreement must be crystal clear. "No room for goof ups. No room for errors," Fob stated, wanting, clarity before he'd lift a finger to work for any man. He was demanding his money must be paid to him in gold. "Gold…I see, and da'on time, hmm," Mr. Utley said standing patiently, facing Fob, smiling with his arms folded. He continued listening to Fob's valueless babbling, saying "Is that so…hmmm I see?" Letting Fob finish talking and when he had heard enough. Mr. Utley then asked, "Are you done? Fob quickly replied. "But of course my good man," Mr. Utley took his time, unfolded his arms, smiled again then he pointed to a sign Fob obviously did not see and said, "You have broken every law posted." Hearing that sudden unfortunate news surprised Fob. He gasped "Hu!" He did not see the sign earlier. Mr. Utley responded by folding his arms again, wearing a stern look on his face and in a deep tone he said, "Shall I send for the authorities?" Already knowing he had the beggar at a disadvantage. Fob knew there was nothing he could do. He looked nervous standing alone on Mr. Utley's property feeling threatened as he stared at the sign again, reading it out loud, this time.

He even read the sign a third time in silence looking for a loophole in the wordage as a means of escape, not finding one he took a hard swallow then slowly whispered, "Nooo, that won't be necessary." "GOOD! Then…we'll start in the horse stables. The shovel is over there! And don't' worry, you'll get use to the smell," stated Mr. Utley. The sign read: Private Property! No Trespassing! No Soliciting! No Pan Handling/ Begging or face fines and Imprisonment. Fob wanted to make a mad dash but didn't. Changing his mind, realizing Mr. Utley had the law on his side and if he had decided to run it wouldn't be long before Mr. Utley, with the law, would have caught up with him, throwing Fob in jail. So he grabbed a shovel and followed Mr. Utley into the stables, unaware but soon to find out, just what Mr. Utley had in store for him.

He worked Fob inside the house with mopping, sweeping, dusting, cleaning windows and sweeping the chimney. Outside he worked painting the sides of an old barn, picking up fallen over-ripen fruit that fell from the trees onto the ground. Fob worked around the sides of Utley's house. He clipped hedges, trimmed trees, bushes, racked leaves, stacked bales of hay he ended his long grueling unscheduled workday by cleaning the stables again. As Fob worked Mr. Utley kept shouting "Hurry Fob the beggar, get it done cause when this sun goes down you won't have any strength to beg another one," Fob fell to the ground from exhaustion. "Hurry Fob, get up!" Mr. Utley shouted. I want to bid you a fond farewell." And he did.

When Fob left the Utley's he could barely raise his head to speak, walk or stand. To him that one day at the Utley's was the longest, strenuous, backbreaking job he had ever worked on in his whole entire life. As Fob tried to walked down the road leaving the Utley's he wobbled and weaved like a drunken man wearing shoes too tight for his feet. He did his best to keep from falling again by keeping his angered mind on Mr. Utley. He was thinking about how Mr. Utley dog treated him. And all the work he put him through, knowing he had no intentions of paying Fob in the first place.

"He didn't have to kick me in my rear end. How was I supposed to know that was his wife or I'd be taking his wallet? Why he tried to work me to death. That fat slimy hog. Oh look! He even made me break my long fingernail too! Wuuu! The nerve of him, how dare he make me give back all that money to his neighbors? Why, they didn't have to turn me upside down shaking the money out of my pockets. I would have given it back to them. If they had asked… Well… I think I would have. Well, any way that's not the point. And what does he mean I'm not a gentleman, who does he think he is anyway? The rich, fat, slob, I'm gonna get him, and get him good! Just you wait n' see the nerve of him!"

Fob thought to himself as he walked with anger, hunger and revenge on his mind. He soon passed Christmas carolers that wanted him to join in their singing. He couldn't. Fob was too worn out. All he could do was shoo them away. He later rested on a fallen tree, eating the fresh pecans from it to help stop his hunger. Walking by a stream he stopped to get a drink of water, but couldn't. His stiff, aching body from his day of work at the Utley's prevented him from bending or stooping. So he continued walking in the direction of town. And it seems every roadside merchant wanted to approach him for purchase of their goods.

Fob said "no" to Christmas trees, roasted chestnuts, hot apple cider and buttered cinnamon pumpkin slices. He was tired of saying '"no" so he simply pulled out his empty pockets leaving them out as a sign of having no money to ward off any other potential asking merchants. People laughed when they saw him coming, especially when they saw a dried sprig of mistletoe caught hanging, dangling from his rear pocket but he didn't care. Fob just kept walking, concentrating on the unfair work ethics he received today.

Then he stopped abruptly in his steps and started to smile. Fob knew right then how he was going to repay Mr. Utley, for nearly working him to death. He rested on several more stops then he headed straight into town. Soon he came upon Nan's gift shop. Fob could see inside the shop window from the road, stopping to reminisce. There she was an old heart throb.

"Ms. Shel'Leese Verlon, "The Singing Ballerina." Aaahh! He sighed. She packed the house back in the days, sold-outs at every theatre. Miss Verlon, the crowned jeweled starlet, performed dancing and singing before kings, queens, ambassadors and people of nobility. "Ahhh, Yes, but that was a long time ago," he sighed stroking his beard reminiscing.

She's aged now. Time has caught up with her. Stricken with gout and nearly penniless, Ms. Verlon is selling her last piece of memories. It was given to her by an admirer of noble birth. It was reported the gent was in the audience that night as he had been every night Ms. Verlon was in town. She gave another one of her stellar performances. He was so taken by her beauty that he lost his composure, leaped out of his seat, reached down, ripping the diamond sapphire brooch off his wife's blouse and threw it on stage to Ms. Verlon. There he stood clapping hysterically, shouting, "Encore!" "Encore!" "Encore!" As his wife sat quiet in her seat, embarrassed. She later tugged on her husband's tuxedo tail for him to collect his composure and take his seat. He eventually did. And later he became more than just an admirer to Ms. Verlon. There were rumors about a child, a male, all though no one knew whatever happened to him or if it was ever true. She's frail now, quiet and old, walking with a limp, trying to hide her twisted fingers with black lace gloves. Doing her best to cover up her widow's hump with a tattered purple wool shawl she found weeks ago. Now, standing inside at the counter of Nan's Gift Shop, silent fighting to keep her dignity and Nan patiently respecting the memories, takes a long time to wait on her because now Ms. Verlon can only talk at a whisper. "My…it's good to see you Ms. Verlon," Nan said reaching across the counter for the colorful butterfly handkerchief filled with Ms. Verlon's past memories. And Ms. Verlon stood on the other side of the counter in silence, reluctant to release them. Her feelings were she needed to give it more thought before letting go of her last memories of passion. Later she slowly slid them across the counter to Nan who stood with a curious look on her face as she untied the small bundle belonging to Ms. Verlon.

"My how pretty" Nan expressed and continued to say, "So colorful the butterflies," as she unfolded the handkerchief. "Goodness! I see you have a beautiful diamond sapphire brooch. Are you sure you want to sell it or trade for something its value?" Nan asked looking at the beautiful sparkling brooch. Ms. Verlon took some time to listen to Nan. Then she replied in a low toned voice. "Well, yes…I just need enough money to sustain me for a month. I am going abroad to live with my family. I only need a little something to hold me until then." "I see, well, I'm sure I can accommodate you ma'am and da' what do you want me to do with these old letters?" Nan inquired… Then amazingly she watched astonished as the face of Ms. Verlon lit up with joy at the sheer mention of those letters. She also witnessed how just thinking of them brought life back into the heart of an old aging woman. Those old yellow faded love letters were from her lover of noble birth… In them he promised to leave his wife for her. Referring to Ms. Verlon as "his rare chosen choice" Nan was able to see that sentence on one of the letters and as she was honored to be waiting on her, Nan couldn't help but wonder, "If the gentlemen ever did," Not wanting Ms. Verlon, to lose the letters. Nan told her she would tightly bundle them together, as she knew they meant a lot to her, knowing they were a precious and intimate part of her life that she would always want to cherish and remember. Ms. Verlon smiled at Nan she nodded her head slightly for "yes" as she waited on her to finish the transaction. Going over to the cash register Nan got out more money than needed giving some to Ms. Verlon. But what Ms. Verlon did not know is that Nan returned her diamond sapphire brooch putting it with extra money inside the beautiful butterfly handkerchief between the love letters giving them back to her. Nan looked at her with a big smile, saying. "Ms. Verlon…I want to wish you a very special Merry Christmas and a special Season's Greetings!" Ms. Verlon was leaning on the counter for balance. She smiled then whispered back," Why, that was nice of you to say. Ms. Nan Sumpter, thank you and the same to you, dear" Upon leaving she noticed the shop Christmas tree, Ms. Verlon stopped to comment on it. "Your tree is so beautiful. Did you decorate it yourself?" She asked. "Oh… No!" Nan happily said. "I had plenty of help." "That's wonderful it sure is pretty. They did an excellent job." "Why, thank you, Ms. Verlon. I'll let them know and it will mean so much to them. Especially knowing that it came from you," Nan replied as Ms. Verlon reached for her love letters inside the tightly bundled handkerchief…"Nan" Ms. Verlon softly called. "Yes," Nan answered. "Did I ever tell you I traveled around the world countless times performing before kings, queens and people of nobility" she whispered. Nan leaned over to hear her then softly replied, "Yes ma'am…you did. And I can only imagine how wonderful that must have been, for you," Nan expressed, gently patting Ms. Verlon on the hand as they both walked towards the door.

Nan watched from the shop window with deep compassion and an opened understanding as Ms. Verlon slowly walked out of view, thinking "What an exciting life she must to have had. What a sad way for it to end." "Oh, Nan… What aisle are your music boxes on. I'm looking for a small one as a gift for my niece. Also I will need for myself about four yards of your fine twined linen in royal blue. Oh! And seven beeswax candles with one wick, in votive style" a shopper asked. "Yes, ma'am" Nan happily said as she went over to assist the lady. Afterward she went back to the counter rearranging the holiday gift basket display, putting more decorations in and on it making it a bit more festive by adding tiny, loose mixed, sparkling faux cut Austrian crystals with shimmering jewels that were deep greens and ruby red. She sprinkled them on the counter next to a glass bowl filled with red, white and green holiday pulled taffy. Nan stood back looking at her holiday gift basket display. She was pleased but added more, fresh cut pines cones with sprigs of mint for fragrance. "Now, that's the added touch I was looking for. That's what it needed." she whispered to herself," When entered an older man smelling like more than one glass of ale, arm and arm with a younger woman. Her cleavage was showing, apparently loosely dressed under her thick faux fur coat with four buttons missing from the top. The young lady was giving the older man a lot of attention, hanging on to his arm, squeezing his arm muscles, telling him how strong he was then trying to reach into his front pocket. While touching something else. "Hey! Watch it! Don't touch that! Don't wake the sleeping giant" He almost shouted. "This ain't the time nor place for that kind of stuff. Now you mind yourself or I'll." He said as he drew back his balled fist to punch her in the face. "Ok! Ok! Gosh, a descent girl cants have any good fun with older coots like you," she said, putting her hands up to her face, protecting it, laughing, then looking down into the glass counter at a Christmas gift for her. The young woman's loud eerie talk and laughter was heard all over the shop. "Whatcha' gonna buy me Puddin'?" laughing she said, knotting and unknotting the long strand of white pearls around her neck, chewing gum, popping it and her fingers moving her body as if dancing to music only she could hear. As she loudly spoke her laughter was carried into the next room where the stranger was seated at a table with Alex and Hilda eating they were also exchanging Christmas gifts. Upon hearing her voice the stranger suddenly stopped laughing at Alex's joke. He immediately turned his head towards the gift shop entrance. Then back at Hilda and Alex sitting at the table. He started to become uncomfortable, fidgety, tapping his fork on the table thinking, talking to himself. *"Now where have I heard that voice before…Where?"* He kept saying, while becoming more agitated and sweaty. His palms started to sweat then he dropped the fork he was holding onto the kitchen floor. Alex quickly picked up the fork for the man, placing it back onto the table. Later the stranger unbuttoned his shirt collar as he displayed rapid breathing, with more sweating. Hilda asked the stranger if he was alright but he did not answer. The stranger was still seated at the kitchen table looking as if to be in a trance. He was trying to remember… tapping his middle finger on the table. "That voice that laugh, where?" The stranger said sitting in his chair, "Where have I …?" he said in a low tone then straightening his posture, starting to sit straight up in his chair, turning his head again towards the gift shop entrance from the kitchen, looking as if he was still in a trance. "Are you alright, sir?" They asked again. But still he didn't hear them. He just kept focusing at the shop entrance. "That laugh!" he whispered. "I've heard it before but…where?" he softly spoke. It appeared the stranger's past events of life were trying to find there place within the present. Seated at the table, his thoughts were swirling before him. His mind was trying to process, understand, sort, decipher. Then, he stood to his feet with small beads of sweat clinging to his forehead, breathing heavy, looking dazed, trying, to figure it out! And, finally! He whispered, *"I know who I am,"* He paused a few seconds then whispered again. *"I'm Sturgis Winters!"* weak, exhausted still breathing heavy. He flopped down into his chair. "Are you okay, sir?" They rushed to ask. "Can we get you something? Want me to call Nan?" Hilda and Alex frightened asked. "Huh? He sighed. He could barely speak at first. "No! Wait," he replied stilled dazed, but then said. "I'm…ah fine," The stranger said almost out of breath. "Wait!" The stranger said feeling for, then grabbing hold to Hilda's hand, stopping her. "No need to bother Ms. Sumpter," he said, still blind, breathing heavily feeling for the cloth table napkin to wipe away sweat from his forehead. But Hilda picked up the napkin first she wiped away the sweat from the stranger's forehead. Later, asking him more questions of concern. "Do you want to lie down, sir?" She asked. "I think you need to lie down," Alex commented. The man paused before speaking then said, "Yes…Yes, I think you're right. I better lie down… this has been a long exhausting day for all of us." "Yes, I agree, sir," Hilda added looking worried. "Would you like for me to get you a cool glass of water before you leave and then help you to your room?" Hilda suggested. "No thank you, Hilda that won't be necessary I can find my way but thank you for asking," The stranger replied as he slowly walked to his room down the hall not letting on to anyone that his memory had returned.

Nan was still waiting on Daggett and his girl as other customers continued to shop, watching, commenting. They were paying close attention to Daggett with his lady friend. "I can have anything I want, remember? That's what you said." Nan tried not to get involved with their merchandise selection but because the young woman was starting to annoy other shoppers. She felt the need to expedite their service by assisting them, to help hurry them out of the shop. "Is there something I can help you with sir?" she asked. "Yeah, I mean yes," he said trying to use correct grammar. "I'm Daggett and this is me, girl. She's new in town aah I would like to see a nice pair of your cultured pearl earrings for her Christmas present. From me of course that matches her necklace or close to it if possible if you can," he answered. "Alright sir…I'll show you what I have in stock," Nan politely said pulling out the earring tray setting it in front of them. His girl looked at the earrings, and frowned, not liking any choices on any trays that were shown to her. So she decided to stroll down the aisles, looking for her own gift while at the same time bumping into customers and not saying, excuse me. Then minutes later they heard these screaming words… "Found it! Oh, Yeah! Oh, yeah! I said, I found it," "Here's what I want you to buy me, Puddin!" she shouted, almost jumping up and down in the shop. She asked Nan to hurry unlock the glass cabinet for her. It was a lady's wrist watch she saw, liked and wanted…it was very expensive. "That's what I want, Puddin! See…right there …See it. There it is see," she said, pointing at an expensive watch inside the glass case, smiling. Daggett looked at the watch, then the price. "Wait a big minute!" he objectively replied, "That will set me back a whole month in wages on the docks. If fen' I get ya that timepiece. I don't know… I don't know about dat one babe," he said, shaking his head no. "Hey you! What ya mean you don't know? You better know or go some place to find out," she shouted, "Now, you listen to this," she continued to say "What happened to the big spender?" his girl loudly ranted, popping her gum in his face. "And what happened to. I give you the world iffen you be my girl," How are you gonna give me this big world iffen you can't even buy me that little tiny watch, me eye," she raged. Daggett stood near the glass case looking nervous. Then again at the price on the watch she had selected. He glanced at other watches in the case, looking for a cheaper watch but he could not find one. In his nervousness he scratched his scalp while the cap was still on his head. Daggett later took off his cap, held it inside his hands, ringing it as if it was wet, then placed it back onto his head.

His girl was still standing next to him still very upset. Shouted, "Well…I thought you said I was your lady and you did say I could have *ANYTHING* in this here shop I wanted, didn't ya?" she yelled in his face. Then he quickly nodded his head up and down for yes…admitting he did say that, but with limits. "With limits," she screamed. "Now YOU…wait just a good minute. Why ya' never talked about limits when ya wants to…" "Aup!" Daggett sharply cut her off needing to quiet her down. She was beginning to really make a big scene. More people were starring, whispering, laughing at the two of them. Nan kept her composure but all the time she was wishing that they would hurry, complete their business transaction and leave. He eventually calmed his girl down by lowering his voice. Along with slowly moving his hands up and down in front of him while he spoke calmly to her. Telling her to relax that he didn't like her costly choice but...he was a man of his word. So he grudgingly bought the watch for her. Nan was relieved quickly telling him that he had made a good choice. That she was sure his lady friend would be happy with her new watch. Nan watched Daggett's lady friend smile as he placed the new watch on her wrist, kissing her. Afterward his woman was feeling really good about her victory. She kissed Daggett again on the cheek, hugging him smiling, giggling, taking her finger to pull a clump of hair on the side of his head near his ear, making a curl. Then telling him how cute he looked which made him start to blush. She felt so good about her victory, and without any cause or reason she wanted to make a sport of someone. "Why not Nan," she thought. Daggett's girl looked at Nan, grinning sarcastically. "Hey, hon...you wants to borrow some of me shades of red lipsticks to liven up your face a bit? Iffen you wants too, you can," she then reached into her purse and pulled out lipsticks, putting them on the counter in front of Nan. At the same time she was nudging Daggett in his side, snickering. "No! Thank you," Nan politely said, smiling at his girl as she gave Daggett his change back from the purchase with the beautiful box it came in. They were just about to leave when his girl decided she wanted to trade a bracelet an earlier beau had given her, for something of value in the gift shop. "Now...how much would you give me for dis pensive bracelet? It was gave to me by a educated, stately man with da expensive proper upbringing," she stated. "Oh, really? That was nice of him," Nan commented, asking her to please remove the bracelet from her wrist so she could properly appraise it. Nan looked closely at the bracelet. Then straight into the eyes of Daggett's girl, saying..."Cheap! Of no value! Common on the street," Daggett burst out laughing. He got the message Nan was sending to his girl right away but it took his girl a while to understand exactly what verbal message Nan was really trying to send her. He began laughing almost uncontrollably. His girl still had not gotten the message. But when she finally realized what was said to her by Nan it bruised her feelings. Nan's timely remarks left Daggett's female friend mad, talking under her breath. Using no repeatable words as the two of them hurried to leave the gift shop. Out front of the shop Nan could see Daggett still laughing almost out of breath, he was laughing between words trying to say something. But Nan was unable to hear this... "Well, Babe, you gotta admit her puss ain't much to look at but you gotta say she got some fancy way with dem words. Aah, come on Babe, don't get too upset they only words." He hugged, kissed his girl trying to cheer her up... "I tell you what ...Why'd don'ts we's go on down to the docks. I want to show off me special girl with dis here new expensive watch I just done bought you," He said winking at her but she refused to go, at first her feelings were still hurt. "Ah, come on Babe let's go make those brawlers with their women down there jealous. What ya say?" Daggett kissed her again on the cheek to coach her into going. "Well...I don't' know." she replied. "Ah, come on Babe don't be like that, do it for me, will ya?" he said but this time puckering his lips

sending her air kisses. "Well…" she said blushing. I don't know,"
almost smiling. Daggett sent her more air kisses which made her smile,
blush a little more. Then she said. "Well, okay, yes, Puddin, anything for
you," "Now…that's me girl. Come on then. Let's go." When they
finally left the gift shop all Nan could think about was. That was one
shopping experience she will never, ever, forget.

The hectic holiday shopping week was finally coming to an end. Hilda
and Alex were waiting on the last customers in the shop. Nan went to
check on the stranger. But before she went Nan hugged Alex and Hilda
wishing them both\ a Merry Christmas, expressing, "Please, don't forget
your pay envelopes. Inside are your special holiday bonuses I hope you
both enjoy your gift," smiling she said. Nan told them to close the shop
up early so they could enjoy their holiday. They smiled telling Nan
Happy Holidays to her as well with each giving her a holiday hug, again.
Then Nan went to knock on the stranger's bedroom door like she always
did before entering but he didn't answer. He was pretending to be asleep
so she softly called out to him again, "Sir," still no answer, so she
quietly opened the door, placed his Xmas gift on the nightstand by the
bed, leaving out of the room. He heard Nan but was faking his sleep as
well as his memory loss. After she left, he quietly got up, to lock the
door then reseated himself in a chair that was in the room. He was trying
to figure out just what happened to him? What caused his injuries along
with his memory loss? And having to come to terms with his present
medical state along with his living arrangements for right now was
secured and comfortable, but he also knew it would not last forever.
After all, his memory did return and it probably wouldn't be long before
his sight returned as well. His convalescent time there allowed him to
listen in on operational procedures of the gift shop. He also learned
about Nan's personal life. That her father was a sea captain who was lost
at sea and he started the gift shop for her when she was a child. She has
no children, no husband, and it appears no male suitor. He also learned
by listening that Hilda helped raised Nan who was an only child. And no
one ever speaks of her mother. The stranger knew he had lucked upon
something good, more like a treasure chest filled with priceless jewels.
Jewels he didn't have to dig beg or hunt for. Every day he overheard
conversations, learning something new about the shop. To him, his
favorite time was at closing. The stranger loved to sit in Nan's rocking
chair wearing his dark glasses waiting for their work day to end listening
for young Alex, the bookkeeper in his eagerness to shout total sales for
that day. He'd sit quiet, grinning, wanting them to think he was resting.
But knowing, realizing he was sitting on a treasure trove. And one
important truth was he knew as of yet Nan had no man in her life to help
her manage the gift shop or run him away.
Sturgis Winters knew whatever he was going to do. He had to act
quickly. So on the following morning he wasted no time in his pursuit
for Nan's affections. With Alex at the orphanage and Hilda at home
celebrating the holidays, Sturgis went to work. He was complimentary

on everything Nan did. He loved telling her about the wonderful fragrance she was wearing. "It captures my attention it stimulates my heart, your lovely fragrance reminds me of someone so fragile, delicate, searching in pursuit of true love." Nan would giggle. She'd blush, especially when he would hold her hand for what seemed like longer than necessary. He even felt his way around the dining table to pull out Nan's chair so she could sit down. He was clever enough to always mention in his conversation with her that he still had no memory or sight, but it was not going to stand in his way in his quest to win her love. Sturgis was cunning. He'd make comments to Nan like, "When my memory and sight returns I know I will find your loveliness in them both." When Nan would hear him say words like those it made her happy she felt warm all over. Especially on the inside she felt like a real woman. But these emotions, feelings were all new to her and Nan was loving it. She felt good, experiencing feelings she had never known before. Nan wasn't use to all that attention, especially from a male. She was hoping she was doing the right things but knew she really didn't know what to do. This whole new encounter with a man was becoming overwhelming to her. And Sturgis could sense it. He was good at his craft, toying with her emotions, confusing her mind, chipping away at her strong will. Sturgis told Nan that he had a surprise for her suggesting first they have an early dinner, ending it with opening a bottle of vintage champagne to celebrate their winter holiday together. He, wanting to surprise Nan by taking her on a winter carriage ride, just the two of them. He knew she loved her town and the people in it and that Nan loved talking about how great it was. He was sure this would be one of his ways of getting closer to her affections. Sturgis sat close to Nan holding her hand on their carriage ride, out and around town. Letting her explain to him about the place where she grew up, often commenting that her lovely voice is so pure, beautiful and descripted. And that she gives him the vivid mental picture needed for when his sight does return. He will already have a clear idea about this wonderful town in which she lives. She shared with him...There was thick, white snow on the rooftops, from the first snow fall of last night. Snow sleighs and ice skates were being enjoyed by kids of all ages.

Even grumpy, old Mr. Humphrey was out in the front yard helping his grandchildren build a snowwoman with the new white fluffy snow. While Miss Geese proudly showed off her young brew of seven colorful, new, winters' down. They too were out enjoying the fresh fluffy snow. There was a quiet stillness in the air. The sky was clear, peaceful for now. Most ponds, lakes and brooks are frozen solid. Meadows that were once green, lush and grassy are now desolated, grey. As it is with most trees this time of the year but some are wearing layers of snow for a beautiful, bright winter canopy. Zines, the artist was at his easel painting another winter master piece for the gift shop to sell. While smaller animals like white winter snow rabbits, owls and winter squirrels that easily camouflage with the white snow are scurrying for food in hopes they will make it back to their homes so they don't become meals themselves. Nan told Sturgis about the fun she had growing up here as a child. And that her friends made her life so well meant that she will always remember by cherishing her childhood herein this special town in which she grew up, well loved. After hearing all the wonderful things about her life here, Sturgis took the opportunity to seize the moment of her joy. He took hold to both of Nan's hands and said. " I can clearly hear the overwhelming happiness in your voice which makes my heart warm with gladness.

Wouldn't it be as equally wonderful to find that same happiness and warmth in someone…you love?" Nan became silent as she tried pulling her hands out of his, but he would not let them go. He picked them up, kissed the inside of them, then suddenly asked Nan for forgiveness for taking the liberty. "Your lovely warmth, welcoming fragrance and beautiful spirit overtook my weak human frailties. I don't know what came over me. Please forgive me, Ms. Sumpter." Nan was dazed, seated in the carriage. She responded by taking a deep breath in then letting it out. Saying, "Well…" "I must admit at this point I really don't know what to think or say. I was totally unprepared caught by surprise at your behavior, but now that I've given it some thought. I believe that under these close confining circumstances it's understandable," As Nan spoke she began to tremble. He could feel her hands were cold, commenting, "Yes, these carriages can be somewhat drafty, chilly," Sturgis said blowing heat from the breath of his mouth into her hands to warm them. "Ms. Sumpter I can feel you're trembling. If you would permit me, I would like to put my arm around you to keep you warm, if that would be alright with you?" smiling he said. Nan was confused. She didn't know what to do or how to think clearly on matters of the heart. She had never been smothered, showered with all this attention before. So instead she quickly reached for the goose down patch quilt that was folded on the opposite seat in the carriage, covering her own lap to keep warm. Sturgis feeling the weight of the quilt smiled saying, "Forgive me Ms. Sumpter I'm afraid you have the upper hand. It seems my limited sight has prevented me from further showing my chivalry as a gentlemen along with my honest intentions towards you. Well, at least let me help you with your covering. And need I say if you were exclusively a part of my life…handmaids would be waiting on your every beck n' call, my lady." As he finished speaking he reached over to help Nan with the covering, slightly brushing his left knee against hers, leaving it there resting on hers for a moment. Nan laughed as she slowly moved her leg, freeing his. But the way she laughed is what he was waiting for. It was then he swiftly ordered the driver to reroute their destination. "To the theatre, driver!" he shouted, "Hurry, the theatre!" Wasting no time Sturgis learned one important rule in life, *"He, who controls the will, controls the mind and the body follows,"* Learning that lesson early in life, he waited, listened for an opening, a weak spot in Nan's voice and it wasn't long before he found it. After gently rubbing against her knee with his, it was that last soft laugh from her. In it he heard something which made Nan vulnerable susceptible to his control. She was lured in unaware taken in by his charm, weakened by his compliments. He overwhelmed, Nan with his verbal pleasantries, almost to, spellbound. And being that naive in this adult stage of life, Nan was no match for Sturgis Winters. She was blinded by all the attention he had given to her throughout the evening. So much so, she couldn't or wouldn't argue against his will or against the last command he gave the driver, "To the theatre," Sturgis shouted. "Hurry!" he demanded. Instead Nan sat close to him in the carriage giving in to more of his romantic advances letting her guard down without even knowing. It was Sturgis who changed the order of their evening by not going to the orphanage as Nan requested earlier. He wanted to and did control their events of the night starting with her home town tour. Later it was the theatre to appease her wishes deliberately, satisfying her every whim which caused Nan not to keep "the promise." But that didn't matter to Sturgis Winters because he was on a mission. Unfortunately Nan missed seeing Alex's performance at the orphanage as she had promised. Alex waited up for her that night with her gift by his side. As he waited he watched the hands on the clock move long pass after midnight, but Nan never showed. That was disappointing to him. And it was the last time he cried himself to sleep.

With everyone back at work, all eyes were on Nan. When not with customers, she would find herself day dreaming, humming, giggling like a young girl of 16 in love. Her mind was always on the stranger, Sturgis Winters. He was still there, but kept his distance avoiding Hilda and Alex as much as possible. Keeping to himself in his room with the door locked or closed. He hid from them staying out of sight, mostly in the back part of the gift shop when they were present. When Nan did not show at Alex's performance at the orphanage on Christmas day as she'd always done in the past Hilda knew something was seriously wrong with her behavior. Even though she showed the following day with his gifts, apologizing, it was still inexcusable and upsetting, not only to Alex, but Hilda as well. Nan's excuse to Hilda was, "I was having such a wonderful evening with the stranger, I forgot about time. It simply just slipped away. And again, I'm sorry," she replied, humming, putting on her new work apron, glowing with happiness. Nan had always been there for Alex, like a mother. But the stranger was changing her. Everyone could see she wasn't the Nan they all knew and to see this change in her was deeply bothersome. Especially to Hilda, who had the most concern since she helped raised Nan, always keeping Nan's best interest along with wellbeing in mind Hilda having her own opinion and suspicions about the stranger kept quiet at least for, now. Her thoughts were. Who was he? What did he want with Nan? So, that afternoon Hilda found herself keeping extra busy, restocking supplies under the counter and on the display shelves. Trying to keep her mind off Nan and that man, it was hard on Hilda, having to deal with Nan's opened involvement with the stranger. So much so that later she found herself whispering, talking to herself repeating… *"I'm going to have a serious reality talk with that young lady …Miss Nan Sumpters, when the time is right."* Words she never thought she'd ever have to say to Nan. And it wasn't long after that statement Hilda got the opportunity. Dr. Laris was concerned that the stranger's optic nerves in his eyes may have suffered damage from the accident. So he arranged an out of town trip for the man to see an eye specialist. Alex accompanied the patient as the ride was far and challenging.

They shared a full carriage riding with a woman, her lap baby along with two small antsy children, which made their trip amusingly annoying but all arrived safely. With the exception of one male passenger a tall, thin man. Having already ridden forty-five minutes into the trip, he demanded the driver to, "Stop, pull over. Let me out of this moving thing!" He shouted then leaped out of the moving carriage, holding on to his toupee` in one hand as he carried the brim of his torn hat in the other. Shaking in his body wearing smeared food stains on his clothing, he screamed, "Madam you must learn to control your children. I've had as much as one can take of that noise coming from those little uncontrollables. I didn't pay my honest fare to listen to all that crying, jumping, moving around. All that commotion coming from them in this carriage not to mention their behavior is intolerable and unacceptable. And… by the way where did you get them from anyway… outer space?" he ranted, having no reply. She, the woman merely turned her nose up at the man from her seat, leering at him though the carriage window, remaining quiet having nothing to say. He was exhausted turning his attention back to the driver demanding a full fare, "immediately," he shouted. The driver merely looked down at the man as he held on tight to the horses' reins. He spoke slow saying, "Well," he paused. Then he continued to speak. "Meet you in the next town, I hope. Another carriage will be coming soon, probably. You'll get your money then, maybe," and rode off. As it did her kids inside the carriage began yelling, making funny faces at the man, throwing their food along with toys and pieces to his crumpled hat, out of the window. Leaving him behind and alone to stand on the side of the road frazzled, bewildered, hoping and waiting for the next carriage to arrive.

Now that the stranger was out of town Hilda confronted Nan about her "misguided" behavior, letting her know that people in town are gossiping about her and what they're saying wasn't very pleasant. "It's necessary that you uphold your reputation. You need to erase, remove, forget everything that prevents you from doing that," Hilda shouted after having tried earlier to delicately discourage Nan from getting too involved with the man. But Nan wouldn't listen. So this time Hilda decided to be a little more forceful, standing in the kitchen drying a set of bone china dinner plates for the gift shop to sell. She opened the conversation with Nan hard getting right to the point. "And Nan, what are you going to do with a man like that?" Hilda used a strong stern tone in her voice as she shouted at Nan. Catching her totally off guard Nan was packing merchandise for the next-day morning dock drop-off. At first she tried ignoring Hilda's antagonizing verbiage not wanting to hear another distasteful word about her house guest. But Hilda wouldn't let up from chastising Nan with words of wisdom regarding the stranger. Nan was tired of hearing it. She stopped packing, sat down on the side of the bed putting her fingers into her ears. She didn't want to hear another negative statement about the man because her mind too was on him, only in a pleasant way. In, her eyes he couldn't be all that terrible not like the way Hilda was trying to depicted him. As far as Nan was concerned he was perfect. The stranger, the man she had gotten used to, and now missed. Being a little reluctant to respond, Nan took in a deep breath then shouted from the next room, "A man like what Hilda?" Hilda waited to answer, having no immediate response. Then she said, "Now, Nan, you know what and who I'm talking about, that stranger who enjoys ruining your family's good name. That kind of man! A man you know nothing about. Like his name to begin or where he comes from." Hilda yelled back, "Don't you realize you're in the midst of an ugly scandal? And there you are being paraded out in the public with him like some cheap, loose, indecent woman! Not to mention your social status. Why you're gambling with your chances of trying to land a good town man, like that successful Sterling Lockhart. We all know he comes from good stock, a good family name those Lockhart's. Why their name is impeccably known throughout this entire region," Hilda continued to say. As she did Nan became quiet, knowing Sterling Lockhart had shunned her earlier this month, confirming it by sending her a correspondence. Nan had gotten up earlier than usual that morning. She was to price sale items for the day. When the special delivery post man arrived it surprised her to see him stop because the shop hadn't opened yet.

Meeting him at the door Nan immediately noticed Sterling's monogram initials S.O.L. on the dark blue stationary. Nan signed for the letter, smiling, opening it to read, in it he stated making it blatantly clear with absolute that *"I, Sterling O'neus Lockhart have or had no intention ever of starting a relationship of any kind with you Nan Sumpter now or in the future. And it would be to your best advantage to stop informing citizens in this town. We do. Furthermore..."* Nan was devastated, grabbing her chest gasping for air, dropping the letter out of her hands onto the floor, leaning onto a table to keep her balance from falling. Trying to put things into perspective and eventually, she did. Nan picked back up the letter and continued reading. She was too hurt, embarrassed to share or tell anyone its content depressed and confused Nan quietly slipped the letter inside her apron pocket as she tried to resume a normal work day. After closing on that day she destroyed his correspondence, keeping the painful words of its contents to herself. While at times often remembering but with, courage she tries to quietly forget. "I've done nothing to be ashamed of. I've don't nothing wrong," she yelled at

Hilda. "Good… you better not have Miss Sumpter, because that was going to be one of my very next questions to you. Nan you have your family's name to uphold!" Hilda shouted getting back to the subject at hand. "And…what about his name, does he remember that, yet? Has he told you anything about himself? Nan, does he remember anything about his family? Huh?" Again, Hilda asked Nan as she placed dried plates down onto the shop counter. Then Hilda put both hands on her hips leaning forward shouting from her belly. "Well, Nan, sense you won't answer my questions. I'll answer them for you. No! No! No! Nan, no, you don't know anything about that man! Well, for all you may know he might have come from a distant planet," Hilda still laughing remarked, trying to catch her breath from laughing so hard. Nan was still in the other room she was not finding what Hilda said as being funny. So Nan didn't laugh. Instead she stopped packing crates for the fourth time. She waited for Hilda to stop laughing so she could go into the same room as her. To talk things out like sensible women without shouting, yelling, or screaming at each other but she changed her mind, again. "Well then…all I can say is that you are a fool Nan Sumpter. A big fool and think about this would you. Have you ever thought he may have a wife with children who's looking for him right now? Have you?" Not having a real defense to that question or any questions Hilda threw at her. Nan decided to listen and think of something serious to say, without talking back right away. She knew Hilda was right. So Nan collected her thoughts and came back strong this time almost yelling, "Okay! Okay! Okay, Hilda, you're right. Yes, okay you're right. I don't know anything about him or his family or his name or where he comes from. But what I do know is that. I need him." "You?" Hilda remarked, fast, quickly and short in her reply to Nan last statement about the stranger. Then the sound of dinner plates crashing, hitting the shop floor breaking into pieces was heard, "You, what? What did you say, Nan Sumpter? You need him?" Hearing those words from Nan startled Hilda. It was Nan's surprised confession about the stranger which caused Hilda to accidentally drop plates that were intended for the gift shop's curio cabinet to be displayed and sold.

Hilda waited a few minutes then asked, "And… What does that mean? You need him?" Nan was a little afraid to speak at first then she began to explain. Speaking slowly to give Hilda clarity but Hilda reply was. "No! Nan… You're wrong. You need that man like I need a toothache. Now, I know you're not thinking clearly young lady," she said sweeping up the scattered, broken pieces of china off the shop floor. "Yes, Hilda I need him!" Nan yelled walking into the same room with Hilda wanting to see what was broken on the floor. And after seeing what was broken Nan became sarcastic, speaking snippet to Hilda. "Well, Hilda it looks as though I'll have to take the cost of those plates out of your wages," remarked, Nan. "Oooh," Hilda replied slow and long. "And da', when did you start that policy, young lady?" Nan not knowing what to say, said nothing. "Well… it's best you don't know the answer to that question Miss Nan. But if you like go right ahead dock my pay, shorten my wages. That won't do you one bit of good and that certainly won't bother me one bit either. Let me also add and it certainly won't make me change my mind about him, that uninvited man who's living here in this shop, right now. Who we all know ought not be." Hilda laughed louder, to make another point. "And sense you brought this matter up. I find it awfully strange you've never docked any of us before for breaking merchandise in this shop. Why, we've all broken items many items in this shop, yourself included. So why would you want to cut my wages now because I've broken something?" Hilda asked looking at Nan, already knowing the answer, still waiting on a reply from her. Nan knew Hilda was speaking the truth about the man but she felt by threating to dock Hilda's wages it was her way of fighting back, showing off. Getting back at Hilda for telling the truth, it was Nan's way of silencing Hilda. It didn't work. It only made Hilda talk louder and longer, adding more words into the conversation than needed. Telling Nan she needs to first start right now by putting a halt to the use of intimidation tactics on her. "Nan, clear your head, put all that silly stuff behind you. Concentrate on what is before you in order to make a very important, non-emotional decision about your houseguest. We've helped him all we can. There's no more we can do for him here!" Hilda shared with Nan. "It's time to let Dr. Laris find him a nice, good place to stay." Nan stood right in Hilda's face, lowering her voice, using her hands motioning them to help express her feelings by saying. "Look. Look Hilda," she said in a soft voice and with great care Nan chooses her words. "Hilda, do you know how old I am, do you?" she asked. Hilda stood back for a moment remembering Nan as a baby. She wanted to smile but didn't. "Child, of course but what…" Hilda started to respond but Nan abruptly interrupted, her saying "Hilda, hush for a moment would you please. Let me speak now would you!" "Certainly," Hilda said. "44 years old. That's how old I am. A woman of 44 years, that has been alone all my life. I had no real life until the stranger came. Now, for the first time in my pitiful existence I'm happy. I'm alive!" she said grinning. "You're alive, Nan," Hilda questioned, "How are you now alive? I thought that's what you've always been?" "Yes, Hilda that is true. I have been but only to a certain degree. And please don't make fun of me Hilda," requested Nan. "Alright, dear but Nan I'm not making fun. I just want to know what you're trying to say?" she stated. "What does that mean, you're alive?" "Well…yes let me explain more will you please? What I mean is that I'm much more alive now than ever before. And do you know why I'm much more alive, Hilda?" Hilda paused then spoke with curiosity, asking Nan, "Why, are you much more alive, now, Nan?" Nan smiled with eagerness to reply. "Because…of the stranger. Because of him," "Oooh, the stranger I see," Hilda slowly sighed. "Yes, that's right, the stranger!" Nan proudly shouted. "And how does that make any sense?" Hilda wanted to know. "Well, it doesn't make any sense to you but to me it makes all the sense in the world. It means a new me Hilda with a new life for me," Nan expressed with happiness.

"I'm, not understanding you Nan. You're talking gibberish," Hilda said. "Well Hilda, let me say it this way then. I didn't have a life before he came, not really." said Nan. "You're still not making any sense child," Hilda replied. "Please, Hilda, if you give me more time to talk it will make sense to you too, you'll see." stated Nan. "Take all the time you need Nan," Hilda sitting down said. "Hilda for years no one really knew how tired I had gotten of being by myself, I hid it well. I used the gift shop as my excuse to consume all of my time and attention but in reality I was really lonely. So one day I made a wish… I went up to the top, stood on the ridge of Mermaid's Bay and there I wished for someone," said Nan "What?" Hilda responded in astonishment. "Yes, that's right! I got tired of being by myself." Nan sternly said. "I wished him here and he came," "What did you say?" Hilda stood to her feet feeling Nan's forehead, checking for a fever. "That's true. I'm not sick, so stop feeling my forehead. I don't have a temperature. I'm fine that's exactly what I did," she said. "Don't be ridiculous you wished him here, ha! Nan I know you don't believe that old fisherman tale, do you?" Hilda quickly commented. "Yes, I do and yes that's what happened. I did wish him here and he came. And now that he's here, he's taken me into an enchanting place. A world I've never known before a place of endless intimacy, gladness, fun, kindness with everything good in it. And everything that's good for me, he gives. I wished all that for myself, Hilda. Why he's given me life again but this time with a whole new meaning. Not like that lonely isolated state of being I was in before. No! No, more of that for me. And now that he's come my heart beats with a true meaning. And you know what Hilda?" Nan asked. "What?" Hilda responded. "I'm going to spend, every breathing moment thinking about him for the rest of my life." Nan said.

Hilda intervened by saying, "Nan, child are you sure you know what you're saying or feeling? Don't you realize this is your life you're gambling with this is not some fishermen tale you heard about over the years. Don't you realize that?" Nan, slow to speak, said, "Well I don't know exactly for sure but I believe that tale. I remember my father telling it to me and I do know this whole thing with the stranger sounds ridiculous but feels right," "It feels right," Hilda whispered. "You have to know more than just that, girl. This isn't some gift shop ornament we're dealing with. This is a real grown man we're talking about, so Nan please stop confusing yourself. Nan your life, your future is too important to fool around with uncertainties," Hilda sternly said adding now listen, "Won't you please give this entire matter more thought?" she added. "Well, Hilda I'll consider it but I can't make you any promises. However, I was thinking as you were speaking and all of what you just said might be true. But wait, Hilda let me ask you a question, may I please," Nan said. "Go on ask me," Hilda replied. "Okay then," Nan said, as she chose her words carefully asking. "Do you know how it feels to be shunned, overlooked or even ignored by men, do you Hilda?" Nan asked. Hilda thought for a moment then replied, "No, Nan sorry I can't say that I have, I don't know that feeling," Hilda answered. "Well, I do Hilda and it hurts. You know Hilda as far back as I can remember as a teen into my adult life. It's always been that way for me. Why I use to think I was one of those hard to sell objects that sat on the shelf in this gift shop collecting dust. Passed over year in, year out, hoping praying someone would take me home invite me into their life. But it never happened. I was so lonely. I use to pretend I had a boyfriend. I'd write letters to him to ease my pain. I still have those letters hidden at the bottom of my cedar chest," Nan confessed. "Oh, Nan dear I'm so sorry I didn't know that," Hilda said with deep compassion. "That's okay Hilda, it's alright, now! Because no more loneliness! Not anymore!" Nan almost shouted, smiling said. "Now, I can finally say and it will be true I have someone special in my life. If only you knew how it felt to tear off another lonely month on my lonely calendar which added up to lonely years of my life. But no more! I'm fed up with being unhappy! Fed up with being alone I'm tired of being lonely," Nan proudly stated. "Nan," Hilda started to speak but Nan cut her words off by saying. "Wait, Hilda! Let me finish… Let me ask you this question," she said. "Go ahead, Nan, ask me" Hilda said. "Is your bed going to be empty, tonight?" Hilda swiftly stood to her feet saying, "How dare you Nan Sumpter. Watch your place young lady!" Nan giggled, and said, "Well mines will. It's been that way all my life," Then Hilda with a bashful face used her apron to fan herself joking saying…"Ha! Well…silly me, if that's all you wanted you know my husband's nephew that ex-prize fighter… if you want to get married." "Stop it!" Nan sharply said. Picking up a gift shop stuffed animal holding it in her arms embracing it with tears in her eyes. Speaking softly, Nan started to smile, saying, "That's not all I want in life, Hilda don't you understand." "But Nan child if you just wait a little longer you'll find the right man that's best suited for you," Hilda pleaded. "I don't want to wait Hilda. I want the man I have now…the stranger I want him!" Nan said. "But Nan," Hilda desperately said. "No! Hilda, the stranger I want the stranger. I like him. I like being with him. Happy like I am with him. Loved by him, thought of first by him, as I am. Why, Hilda when I'm with him I feel so very different. More than special, you know he smothers me with attention, affection and romantic conversation. Mmmm humm he does, Hilda, smiling Nan admitted "Why, Nan!" Surprise, Hilda commented. Nan went on speaking about the stranger, expressing "I can't explain it in words but when we're together we feel so enraptured. As if he and I are one being in this whole big entire planet with him treating me as if he's stolen the love from the hearts of every woman on this earth. And gave it to me…And you know what Hilda? I love that feeling."

As Nan spoke Hilda was moved by her innocence's taking her apron, wiping tears from her eyes, knowing despite of all Nan's happiness. She knew in her soul that the stranger was no good for Nan. Making one last ditched effort to change her mind about the man. As Nan walked toward the door to leave, Hilda shouted. "Well… What are you going to do when his sight returns, huh?" Nan froze in her steps. With her right hand still on the doorknob she turned slowly to face Hilda, saying. "And just what, do you mean?" Looking her right in the eyes, Hilda dropped her head slightly, lowering her voice, looking away. Hesitant was Hilda to speak, then she said, "Well, he has a right to know. That's all I was saying." Nan lowered her chin to her chest, waited, raised her head and expressed. "Hilda, he'll love me for who I am as I love him for who he is." But before the door completely closed, Hilda yelled out loud, again. "Nan Sumpter, a man like that is only going to break your heart. So get ready to sweep up the pieces!" But Nan didn't stop. She kept walking in silence out the shop door not looking back at Hilda or listening to anything else Hilda might have to say. Nan's heart, mind and thoughts, were on the stranger, as she was content in her quest, her pursuit for love.

Somewhat frustrated, Hilda went back to put the boom into its corner closet. She tried to dry her tears while blowing her nose when in walked Mr. Toliver the post man. "Good day! Good day! Ms. Hilda, how are you doing, today? You know I called out to Ms. Sumpter but she didn't answer. I saw her talking to the constable I hope everything is alright with her? Can I get you something Ms. Hilda you look a little upset. I hope everything is okay with you as well?" He inquired. Hilda made up a quick excuse. "Oh, I'm okay. Everything is fine. Just a little gout flare up that's all. But thanks for asking. "Oh, you're welcome. You know I heard those can be quite painful," he replied. "Yes, they can," said Hilda changing the subject to. "The authorities are here today making their presence known in this business area to keep the askers away. We're hoping with them here it will stop the beggars from bothering our customers. The authorities are acting more as a deterrent than anything else. Promising to come by more often just to check on things around here, boy we're glad to see them too," said Hilda. "Well good then! Give Ms. Sumpter my best, would you please," stated Mr. Toliver "I sure will," she said sitting near the counter, stamping incoming mail along with reading names on parcels, packages that were delivered to the shop by him, making sure it was their mail. "Oh! Before I forget Eshman's Bakery from down the street sent over a complimentary loaf of fresh baked buttered bread. As a thank you gift, I'll go get it. I left it outside in my mail cart. And it's still nice n' hot," smiled Mr. Toliver walking out the door. Then Hilda decided it was now a good time to get up and pour two cups of hot tea. She knew Mr. Toliver was on a rigid time schedule. So when he would reenter the gift shop they could quickly resume talking. "Oh, that was so nice of Mr. and Mrs. Eshman. I'll have to return the favor. And you are right this loaf of bread is still nice and hot!" Hilda said smiling, further saying. "You know Mrs. Toliver I think I'll take them over a few boxes of Nan's chocolate candy before I leave the shop today," she happily remarked as they continued chatting about the upcoming Governor's Ball. Hilda wanted to know if he had delivered any ball invitations as of yet. "No. Not yet," he replied, sipping his tea. Neither expressed, but I'm sure both were thinking, hoping, wouldn't it be wonderful if Nan finally did receive an invitation to this year's ball, since she has always been overlooked so many times in the past. "I'm keeping my fingers crossed," Mr. Toliver was thinking. Then he shared with Hilda, "I think it still a little too early to tell. Who will actually be attending this year's ball, hopefully I should be delivering invitations in the mail to all attendees, very soon," he told her. And he was also quietly hoping Hilda would finally be getting one as well. "Oh, well. Thanks for the few minutes of rest. I enjoyed the cup of tea," he commented, putting his mail cap back on his head. "Hey! Ms. Hilda you want to hear something funny?" he asked. "Why of course Mr. Toliver," she answered. "As I was leaving out the door this morning my wife told me to slow down. Stop working myself feverishly." "Oh…she did and what did you tell her?" Hilda chuckling asked. "I told her I can't do that. I wouldn't know what to do with my fidgety self." They both shared in on laughing. Then Mr. Toliver glanced down at his watch, he took a few more swallows of tea. "Oh boy…I really gotta run. If, I hurry Hilda I have just enough time to finish my mail deliveries," "I understand Mr. Toliver, do give Mrs. Toliver my best will you, please," "Yes, ma'am I sure will and thanks again Ms. Hilda, see you tomorrow." "Yes, tomorrow," Hilda repeated standing to remove tea cups off the counter then she made her way into the kitchen. And for some unknown reason she decided to stop, take a look out of the kitchen window. Then Hilda smiled as she watched Mr. Toliver, scurrying, happily down the street whistling, pushing his mail cart tipping his cap to ladies along the way as the sun began to set.

Each day the stranger was gone Nan inconspicuously watched for his carriage to return, she missed him so much. That there were days Nan wouldn't eat. When asked by Hilda. "Why aren't you eating your meals? They're perfectly good. I prepared them myself. And they've all been your favorites, too?" Nan would later make up excuses telling Hilda she didn't have an appetite because she was tired of eating the same old food. She would mope around the shop all day doing nothing. Then there were nights she didn't sleep, waking up the next morning cranky, blaming the mattress for being too hard, as the reason for her not sleeping well. "Odd you'd said that Nan," Hilda told her cleaning the shop windows. "Why, you've been sleeping on that same mattress for years. This is the first I've ever heard you complain about it being too hard. That's strange wouldn't you say?" She knew and could tell Nan missed the man but Hilda also knew the strong feelings Nan had for the stranger wasn't right. Hilda was afraid to comment too harshly again about him she wanted to keep down the bickering between the two of them at least for right now.

But Hilda was more concerned about Nan not eating or sleeping knowing overtime it could possibly affect her good health. Instead Hilda observed Nan by paying closer attention to her behavior, now that the stranger wasn't around. Her personality, it was different, like her old self again. "Our Nan is back," Hilda happily thought to herself seeing the change in her. But that was just an outside observation. Inside Hilda couldn't begin to imagine how Nan's lonely heart ached for him. It was empty. She needed and missed him. She longed for the stranger. And to her his carriage couldn't come soon enough. Nan tried her best to keep busy and not think or daydream about him. Seated at the table she had just completed the inventory count of polished silverware, keeping her mind occupied with things to do. Hilda was busy fussing as usual about the inventory stock. "We need to start back working on it. It's becoming backlogged, again. We need to make more room for the merchandise we already have. Speaking of which… What about those whaler harpoons sitting back there near those opened sea chests? They've been in the same place for an awful long time, now all of that stuff has? She stated. "Where, what harpoons?" Nan asked. "Back there," Hilda said pointing to an inventory room in the back shop area. "Oh, that room, those harpoons," Nan quickly replied. "Aren't they still back there collecting dust along with taking up much needed space?" Hilda inquired. "Why, yes, you're right. I think they are. Hilda, but you do mean the ones that are in the second stock room leaning up against those stacked wooden barrels of rum that washed ashore months ago. Are you talking about those?" Nan asked to be sure. "Yes, those…" Hilda answered, further saying, "And clearly no one working here is going to ever use those harpoons to catch a whale or anything else of that size. Besides I harpooned my chubby husband years ago," she stated laughing, making a joke doing her best to cheer up Nan. And it worked! Nan smiled. She even laughed a little, commenting, "Oh no, Ms. Hilda that's where you're wrong. I can remember back to then and he wasn't chubby years ago," she said laughing. "True," Hilda replied then added. "I fattened him up just for me and he loves it," They both laughed. Hilda later changed the conversation back to, "Now let's not forget those crates sitting back there next to that spinning wheel filled with yards of ribbon, fine silk and lace. Not to mention those bolts of colorful fabric, still in good shape locked in several sea chests somewhere in that back room. Why, I remember the day when all that stuff

washed ashore. Merchandise that should be up front so customers coming into the shop can see and buy them. We can't make money from merchandise if it's sitting back there unseen, now, can we?" she sternly stated standing at the stove plating her dinner putting it on the table. "You're right," Nan was uninterested but agreed. As she raked her green peas around the plate with her fork not really wanting to eat. Her interest was in seeing the stranger. But to appease Hilda she added. "I agree with you Hilda. We can start moving those items out front tomorrow. Along with the rest of the merchandise that's been sitting back there in the way," she said.

Then the shop bell jingled. It was Alex and the stranger. Neither Nan nor the stranger had to say a word. Nan dropped the fork she was holding in her hand onto her plate and stood to her feet. The look on both of their faces told the story. She and the stranger missed each other, embracing, kissing forgetting everyone else was in the room. Hilda along with Alex stood back and watched looking baffled, not knowing what to do or say. Later that night the stranger proposed to Nan. Removing his dark glasses, he got down on one knee, using her silk yarn to fashion a circle for a wedding ring and said, "Miss Nan Eloise Sumpter. My absence from you made my heart realize that you are my soul, the reason I exist. May I have the honor of asking you to marry me, becoming my wife, Mrs. Sturgis Winters?" Nan was shaking with joy as Sturgis held her hand, kneeling down to propose. Having tears of gladness in her eyes she said, "Yes! Yes! Oh, yes!" And as clever as it may seem he, Sturgis Winters knew in all the excitement Nan would never think to ask him, "When did your memory return?" Telling Nan his wedding gift to her was his returned memory, with him adding more to the conversation, expressing, "This, wonderful celebrated moment. "Right Now" we will both always remember sharing it together as we embarked upon it as one life. One soul as husband n' wife for the rest of our lives, together now and forevermore," he announced. Nan was overjoyed! Sturgis was right. In all the celebrated excitement Nan forgot to ask him…when did your memory return but to her it didn't matter because she was getting married to the man she loved. His memory had returned. He knew his name but most importantly she knew his name. Sitting not far from Nan, was Hilda, she witnessed the proposal, too. But as he spoke Hilda wasn't at all ecstatic about seeing or hearing it. While he was speaking Hilda thoughts were…a mouth full of fancy words for a foolish heart. However, she was glad for Nan's new happiness, but Hilda reserved the right to keep her true opinion about the man Nan was marrying to herself. Allowing peace to flow by remaining silent. So, she decided it was best to share in on Nan's joyous occasion by toasting the new couple's life together. It was then Sturgis insisted that he and Nan marry the following day, having a small wedding ceremony. Near the end of their wedding services Hilda was overheard saying, "Happiness comes in many different ways. I truly hope Nan has finally found hers because that would have made her father very happy." And it seems as if she did. In attendance was only Nan, Sturgis, the parson, the parson's wife and Hilda. Young Alex did not attend. Nan's wedding was the talk of the town. In the town in which she grew up "her rushed wedding" was discussed at dinner tables, shops, pubs even restaurants. It seemed everyone was talking about "the man from the sea and Nan" With all the idle gossip, talk circulating around town about Nan and the man from the sea. It still did not douse the true romance between those two. The newlywed's honeymooned at "Cottage Cove" a beautiful reclusive area on the beach which is popular with married couples around the globe. The breathtaking views of Cottage Cove were splendorous and enchanting with unsurpassed beauty. It is known for and it has been said only nature knew true love, with romance and passion, beckoned there. Especially in winter season, it was stunning. A picture-perfect snow lit view from their cottage window, which promised and fulfilled days that were quiet, beautiful with anticipated nights that glistened with soft, fresh falling, majestic, wind driven snow that dressed the morning landscape with elegances.

Fireplaces filled with burning cedar, pine logs and dancing ambers released a sweet fragrance that filled the entire cove. Most newlyweds like the Winters' were seen only a few times from their balcony. They shared most of their time inside, together. Nan and Sturgis enjoyed their privacy. Their marriage was consummated the first night. Taking many romantic handheld walks during afternoon and at evening hours along the cove where she vividly described to him the magnificent winter landscape. Stopping on occasion, chatting with other newly married brides and grooms, each, proud to show off wedding rings. While having whimsical marriage proposal stories to share. Although Nan was delighted at her wedding ring selection she was hoping her husband Sturgis when his sight returned would be equally delighted as well. Once back inside their warm cozy cottage after enjoying one of many splendid meals, Sturgis decided to show a side of humor. Feeling for Nan's body, picking her up in his arms, saying, "The meals we were served were amazing and delicious but they can't compare to my wife's excellent culinary skills." Sturgis said. As he put Nan down then rubbed his stomach, shouting. "My dear your meals are always outstanding fit for a king and his loving queen my Lady," He taking Nan's hand kissing it, bowing, laughing as they both embraced each other kissing beaming with happiness. Yes, these along with other delightful, intimate moments Nan shared here at Cottage Cove, where love does truly beckon. And as for Nan these priceless moments she will always want to remember. They will be etched in love for the rest of her life. A life she has finally found with a man that gives her complete satisfaction.

With the honeymoon coming to an end, Nan and Sturgis cuddled their closest during the night. Sitting by the fireside, sipping champagne, watching golden ambers pop, swirled, danced from the last logs burning in the fireplace. They followed the newlywed tradition at Cottage Cove by leaving their Bride and Groom champagne glasses resting on the fireplace mantel touching, side-by-side, base down for good luck, a happy marriage and a quick return. Nan with Sturgis was just about to board the morning carriage to depart. When Nan waited a few seconds before completely stepping on she took a long sentimental moment looking back at Cottage Cove, wiping away tears of joy, but keeping the memory of knowing that true love, passion with pleasure was shared there. A time she will always want to remember and never forget.

Once inside their carriage Nan sat very close to her husband kissing him, smiling, beaming with marital bliss. As the newlywed's carriage rode off heading into town in the direction of the gift shop. The drive into town was a windy one. Their carriage moved often with the breeze. The driver had to pull over twice to fix a loose wheel he also had to remove large pieces of debris from off the road. He apologized for any inconvenience but it still delayed their arrival time. Hilda, Alex and Abby, Hilda's niece, eagerly waited for the bride and groom to arrive. The three of them faithfully ran the gift shop while the new couple were honeymooning. Wedding gifts, cards along with letters of congratulations from well-wishers continued arriving. Mrs. Utley was near the area so she decided to hand-deliver her gift to the couple personally. Hoping to be the first to meet Nan's new husband, but their carriage arrived too late. Mrs. Utley grew tired of waiting, so she expressed, "Hilda, do tell Mr. and Mrs. Winters I was here today and am taking my wedding gift back with me. Perhaps I will return tomorrow attempting once again to personally hand deliver it to them, if I'm in the area." Hilda too was also tired from the long wait, so she replied, "That will be fine, Mrs. Utley do what pleases you," to that Mrs. Utley remarked. "Why, thank you, Hilda. I always do!" Mrs. Utley said then, hurried out of the door with Nan's wedding gift in hand, to meet her husband for dinner. At first Hilda was a little upset because Mrs. Utley refused to leave Nan's wedding gift with her as everyone else had done. But Hilda later realized no need in upsetting herself behind Mrs. Utley's behavior because Mrs. Utley is going to be Mrs. Utley regardless. And no one can change that. It was late, way into the night when the Winters' finally did arrive. The shop was closed. All lights were off inside. Everyone had gone for the day. On the following morning riding to work Hilda's thoughts were Mr. and Mrs. Winters will still be too exhausted from their long trip. They will most definitely be in bed asleep when I arrive. She had already made up in her mind not to wake them for any reason. But to Hilda's surprise when her carriage pulled in front of the walkway, Nan with her husband was up. They had already opened the shop for business Hilda was happy, glad to see them. She was thinking when Alex and Abby come they will be glad to see them, too. Hilda couldn't believe they were up so early. Nan hugged her with happy tears in her eyes. Then Alex and Abby came running up the walkway excited to see Nan. They all waited to shake Sturgis' hand, congratulating him again and you could see the new bride was filled with love and excitement. She was truly a blushing bride. While Nan and Sturgis were gone the gift shop ran smoothly, but today it was extremely busy for the newlyweds. The shop was filled with early morning shoppers which made the hours fly by and as it was coming towards the end of the work day. Still it was a constant flow of new customers. Some came to shop. Others to look at Nan's new husband, the rest came to browse, but all who came before leaving gave happy congrats to the new married couple. From the window you could see the Brighttens carriage pull up. Neals with his sister Olivia Brightten they came to pay for their mother's purchases. She ordered several days ago. Her list consisted of many items which included several cases of aged cognac, crystal stemware sets, antique porcelain cup and saucer sets along with a few more bulky items. Hilda assisted them while they got a chance to meet Nan's new husband, congratulating them both. "My, he's not only charming behind those dark glasses, he's gorgeous. Nan! You better watch him." Olivia said, admiring Nan's husband. Olivia Brightten was gracious, appealing, an astute scholar, a well-known socialite with alluring captivating green eyes that were focused on Sturgis. Hilda stood back watching, listening as she waited on the Brighttens. For the first time she could see Nan's insecurities. They were visible. And Nan was looking for a way, a place in which she needed to hide them. If her insecurities, were obvious to Hilda they were also obvious to Olivia as well.

The remarks Olivia made about Sturgis Winters were true. She didn't lie. But her remarks about Nan's husband made Nan feel uneasy, defenseless, challenged in her own fears. And for the first-time Nan felt what it meant to be afraid of losing her husband to another woman.

Standing at the end of the counter waiting on Hilda to come with his change was Neals Brightten, Olivia's youngest brother. He was always polished, groomed, flamboyant, well dressed…an aristocrat. With a family name that is known around the world, yet to him he was still unaware he carried the male family secret. That was passed down to him from his great-grandfather on his mother's side. Hilda finally arrived with his change. Then suddenly he decided to have the items delivered instead, saying, "I had no idea mother ordered so much," which made Hilda have to rewrite the order. Even Neals himself added more items to the list. Then later becoming impatient as he had to wait for Hilda to finish the order. In his wait, he stood and removed his soft blue suede hat, light-blue gloves tapping his dark mahogany cane on the shop floor. Neals also checked inside his satin suit jacket pockets making sure to have brought his silver flask with the family crest engraved on front in black diamonds. His sister Olivia then extended an opened invitation for the couple to attend a charity luncheon held at their mother's estate every 3rd Saturday of the month. "It's more like a social gathering to raise money for the orphanage," she said. She then told them they could pick up their wedding gift at the same time. Between yawns Nan tried coming up with excuses, but Olivia wouldn't hear of it. Eventually she gave in accepting the invitation, telling Olivia, "I can't promise exactly when we will attend but we will try to come soon." "Splendid!" Olivia said. "I'll inform mother she'll be delighted and do come casually dressed," she happily said, standing next to Nan with her interest on Sturgis. Hilda hurried coming from the back with the completed order, thanking them both saying, "You can expect the delivery tomorrow at noon." Hilda continuing to speak asking, "Is there anything else I can help the both of you with?" They looked at each other and said. "No, Ms. Hilda but thanks for asking," "Good then," Hilda said, looking at Neals and he smiled back at her putting down the small glass bottled ship that rested on the counter. Then he turned again to his sister and said, "Olivia, mother will be thrilled hearing this information. First, she'll have her order just in time for the next social gathering. And second, the Winters' will be attending one if not all of mother's social gathering. Isn't that wonderful! I'm delighted for both I know mother will be too," he commented. "Remember…Dress casual," Olivia repeated, to Nan and Sturgis walking towards the door. "And Nan Winters get some rest would you please," Olivia said smiling. Nan yawned covering her mouth, shook her head up and down in agreement with Olivia's statement. They were pleased with the choice of having their mother's order delivered but once outside. Neals stood close to his sister speaking, "My dear sister…don't you think they make an interesting couple, wouldn't you say, sis?" She looked at her brother took him by the arm, not commenting. As they walked to their carriage Olivia was thinking in spite of her brother's remark she was happy, glad for Nan's marriage to Sturgis. But deep inside of her, she was wishing it was she that should have found and married the man from the sea handsome Sturgis Winters. "Come on Neals let's go! We can't be late. Mother is expecting us to be on time," she told her brother as their carriage speeded off.

With the Brighttens gone the shop was empty. Alex and Abby went into one of the back inventory rooms to work on the merchandise backlogged orders. Hilda thank them again expressing, "The work you two are doing back here today won't help us catch up. But will help us out a great deal, making a big difference! Thanks again, you two," Hilda stated. She later told Abby, "After you've logged in a few more items with this being your last day you may leave early if you like." "With pay I hope," Alex remarked smiling. "Yes, Alex with pay," Hilda laughed said, leaving going into the front part of the shop to insisted that the newlywed's go back to bed to get some rest. "Nan Winters you're not doing us one bit of good yawning all over the place…off to bed, the two of you. Off! Go ahead! Off!" Hilda raised her voice pointing to the bedroom area. "Okay! Okay!" Tired with fatigue they both said. Neither Nan nor Sturgis argued with that strong demand given by Hilda. "And get some rest this time!" she said laughing. "We can handle running this shop, again." No sooner than Hilda sent them off to bed the shop bell rang. Nan had an unexpected visit from Nathaniel, a breeder of horses. A lover of chess, and a lover of Nan's exquisite chocolate candy, of which no one knows the recipe but Nan. He was in town on banking matters. Hilda sees him walking through the gift shop door. "Well, hello Mr. Kingsly!" she happily said. "Well… Hello, Ms. Hilda. But first here is Nan's wedding gift," he said waiting a moment to speak. Then he said with a big smile on his face, "Now… Do you know why I'm here?" Hilda chuckled. "Yes I do! How many boxes can I get you?" "Oh, I'll need eight but can you gift wrap four of them with birthday wrapping?" he asked. "You bet cha Mr. Kingsly. Wait here. I'll be a minute. It's some hot tea on the table over there. Help yourself." "Why thank you Ms. Hilda," he said, walking towards the table to pour, himself a cup of tea. Nathaniel Kingsly a top breeder of rare Arabian horses. When once asked by a spectator, "How do your horses out perform their competitors?" In which he replied, "I credit their outstanding performance to the lush, green, rich vegetation near Stross' pumpkin patch where we live. They thrive on the bluff's mineral rich foliage. They love that stuff up there. And yeah, it seems to be working in their favor," Mr. Kingsly remarked with a smile, further saying, "Yes, I think that does have a lot to do with their winning success, wouldn't you agree?" He remembered sharing that conversation with spectator's years ago as he stopped to look at a first place trophy that was on one of the shelves inside Nan's shop. Mr. Kingsly spoke very candid with Hilda as he walked down shop aisles browsing enjoying his cup of tea while she wrapped his boxes of candy. He also wanted to congratulate the wedded couple on their marriage, asking Hilda if they were back from their honeymoon. She told him "yes" but that he just missed them because she told the love birds to go back to bed for some badly needed rest. "You know they had a long, tiring, trip home last night. I told the Winters' not to worry just go back to bed," Hilda said. "That was so nice of you, Ms. Hilda" Mr. Kingsly replied. "Oh, I don't mind helping out where I'm needed," she said thanking Mr. Kingsly again for Mrs. Winter's wedding gift. Telling him she would inform them both that he had dropped by. And him, unable to wait Mr. Kingsly started walking then stopped in his steps, after opening a box of Nan's chocolate candy that was intended for the long ride back home. He picked up a piece, held it in his hand, smiling looking at the chocolate, savoring in its delightful chocolatey aroma… Waiting for its delicious anticipated taste …Then he took a bit. "Mmmmm…" he said further commenting with a smile. "This chocolate is uninterrupted goodness," adding "I tried to wait! You saw me Hilda…" he said almost giggling "I just couldn't

wait. I had to have a bit. I love this stuff! I can't get enough of it but of course you already know that already," He said, smiling further. "You know Hilda, Nan's chocolate candy always delights my sense of taste with its fresh, rich, lingering chocolate aroma. And how does she make this stuff taste so good?" He said looking at Hilda smiling and she looked back at him, agreeing, shaking her head up and down for yes, trying not to laugh. He took another bit, expressing. "This chocolate candy" Mr. Kingsly said, showing Hilda the opened box. Mr. Kingsly continued to speak. "Is so soft, silky, a smoothness of indulgences which satisfies my chocolate desires. Again, I must say. I love this candy!" he stated, chewing, smiling carrying the unopened boxes of chocolate candy under his arms walking towards the door. Almost to step outside Mr. Kingsly turned himself around to face Hilda and shouted at her in a deep bellowing laugh, "And I love a damn good game of chess, too," he said going to his carriage that was pointed in the direction of the bluffs. Hilda stood at the doorway smiling, waving goodbye, trying not to laugh but knowing with exact understanding what Mr. Kingsly meant about the delicious taste of Nan's chocolate candy.

The day wasn't too rushed for Hilda or Alex. They managed to wait on every last customer without Nan's help. It was near closing time when Penny rushed into the shop, leaving her dog outside, breathing hard from running all the way. She had seen a cloth doll in the gift shop window weeks ago, "Do you still have it? Huh do ya Ms. Hilda?" She said huffing and puffing, almost completely out of breath. "Have what, child?" Hilda said looking at Penny puzzled. "You know…the little cloth doll you had in the window not too long ago. Do you have any left?" Hilda paused a minute thinking before speaking, "Oh, wait Penny you mean that doll. Well…let me go see. If we still have any left. You know Penny they sold out so fast the last time we had them in. I think they're all gone." Hilda told Penny to sit down, catch her breath, "And lace your shoe too before you slip and fall." Alex intervened being very candid in saying, "Yeah, before you slip, fall AND break your neck! Those dolls are all gone Penny remember I told you last week we didn't have anymore," he said standing behind the counter, putting sales receipts in order. "Yes, I think you're right Alex," Hilda said as she stopped walking towards the storage room. Where the dolls are kept, she further said. "Why, yes, Alex come to think of it and now that you've mentioned it. I haven't seen any of those dolls around here but I'll go check for you Penny just to make sure." Hilda took off again towards the back stockroom to look for the doll. "I already told you last week we don't have any more of those dolls," Alex, again said. "Oh, you hush Alex you don't know everything there is to know," Penny remarked. Then moments later she asked, "Hey, Alex you want me to wait for you?" she asked, Alex while picking up, holding in her hands smiling a new stuffed animal looking at it with interests but really wanting the doll she came into the shop for. So she placed the stuffed animal back onto the shelf. Later she sat back down. "No, thanks that's okay, Penny," he answered. Hilda didn't come back right away but when she did she came back smiling. "Oh… Look! Yes, we did have one. And this is the last one. My, aren't you lucky Penny." "Oh! Boy thanks, Ms. Hilda!" Penny stood to her feet elated. "Thank you, again! No need to wrap her, she's for me!" "See Alex, see I told ya! Naaa!" Penny joked with Alex looking at her new doll smiling. "To finish answering your question you asked me earlier, I have to help Hilda close the shop. It was just the two of us at work most of the day." said Alex. "Abby left early and Mrs. Winters was resting in today," he said. "But go ahead try to save me a seat at the dinner table if you can. I can't leave now. I have the shop's bookkeeping to do along with restocking unsold merchandise and other job duties," "Gosh! Alex, you have to put all that stuff away? And do all of that before you can leave work, tonight" Penny asked. "Yes, I sure do," Alex replied. "Gosh," she sighed looking at Alex's job duties for the night. But right in the middle of his conversation with Penny, Alex changed his mind. He asked Hilda if he could walk Penny to the orphanage, he'd be right back. Hilda stopped what she was doing, took an unusual look at him then she said with a smile on her face. "Why, yes Alex, you may," Hilda later stated, "You know Alex, I'm proud of you.

You're growing up!" "Huh?" he responded putting on his jacket, not quite understanding exactly what Hilda's statement was all about. But Hilda did. She also knew soon in life young Mr. Alex would too. Alex was putting his cap on his head going out of the door looking confused he was still trying to figure out what Hilda meant. Then Penny looked at him commenting, "Oh, don't worry yourself silly about it now, Alex. You're still young, let's go!" He with Penny walked slowly to the orphanage both shared their life aspirations with each other, when surprisingly she said. "Gosh! Alex, do you think we're asking a lot?" Penny really wanted to know. Then he looked at her replying. "No…Penny I don't think so. Why'd you ask?" he inquired. "Ooof good, Alex," she sighed, saying, "Because what we want to make our dreams come true is so much. We'll need a lot of time on our side to get it all accomplished. And we may even have to borrow time from somebody to get all this done, wouldn't you say, so Alex?" After Alex heard that from Penny, he stopped walking turned to face her putting his hand on her shoulder saying, "Now, look here Penny, come on now just how real is that statement. Borrow time from somebody…now really?" Penny took a few seconds to think about what she just said. Then she looked up at Alex trying not to smile or laugh. She started to smile, a little, then a lot. Later they both burst out laughing as they continued their walk, with Alex joking from time to time commenting, repeating Penny's words, "Borrowing time from somebody. Now, really Penny, please,"

The next day's sky was clear. Nan was bringing in the morning paper. She had gotten the much needed rest at Hilda's request, so it was back to business for her. With the honeymoon now over she had a gift shop to run. Things ran pretty normal with a few exceptions. Sturgis came to the front part of the shop while it was free of customers. He informed Hilda and Alex they were to no longer refer to his wife as Nan, but as Mrs. Winters, effective immediately. The two of them were stunned Hilda had to sit down to think things out asking herself, "What brought this on? Why would he demand this request from us?" Hilda said, whispering to herself commenting. "Mr. Winters' request was more of an insensitive demand. When he was done speaking, Sturgis left the room leaving them to ponder his demand "Hmmm, I wonder if Nan is aware of this demand," She further thought. Nan couldn't comment. She was outside in the stables when Mr. Winters approached Alex and Hilda strongly making his request known to them. Hilda kept quiet. She did as she was asked. The name change was difficult at first because it had always been "Nan" around the gift shop and nothing else. It took some time getting use to but they managed meeting the request of Mr. Sturgis Winters. However, it still didn't sit well with Hilda, she had more quiet concerns wondering what other unfavorable changes was he secretly implementing around the shop with Nan's love-struck approval. It was obvious the mood in the gift shop changed from cheerful and peaceful to bitterness with resentment toward him but as the days progressed things changed for the better. It was on a Thursday, Nan with her new husband stepped out to have their first lunch in the public as Mr. and Mrs. Winters, dining at a well-known local, restaurant in town. They received warm congratulatory wishes from most neighbors and friends who came over to their table to wish them well. One in particular was Mr. Ethen Utley. They were unaware he was in the restaurant. Coming over to acknowledge them, Mr. Utley was sincere in his congrats on their marriage. He also brought over to the table with him a little humor, sharing with the newlyweds several martial jokes. Leaving Nan and Sturgis laughing to tears, he returned to his table sending over his wife. She arriving at their table immediately announced. "Well, good afternoon Mr. & Mrs. Winters! Finally, it's my turn," Mrs. Utley said, taking in a deep breath then clearing her throat before speaking next. "Well, how wonderful for the two of you and let me be one of the first to wish you both my sincere best in your married life together." Nan and Sturgis sat looking at Mrs. Utley they were surprised that she was there, too. Then the Winters' replied, "Why, thank you Mrs. Utley for your kind words." They also informed her that Mr. Utley just left their table congratulating them too. She replied. "Yes… I know that too. So, this is the handsome mysterious, Mr. Incognito man we've all heard so much about," she said. "No, Mrs. Utley, this is my husband Mr. Winters," Nan replied. Mrs. Utley ignored Nan's remarks she went right on speaking, "I stopped by the shop weeks ago to give the two of you your gift but I refused to leave it because I didn't want someone to put a price tag on my expensive gift I brought for you. Then resell it for a profit, you do know that could happen. So I took it back home with me," she jokingly replied. "But don't worry I will come again soon. Oh, Nan by the way did my dwarf Yew and Baobab trees arrive, yet?" "Yes, they did Mrs. Utley," Nan answered. "What about my signature orchids?" "Yes… as a matter of fact. They arrived just this morning," Nan answered. "Good then! I'll come by one day next week to pick them up. And at the same time drop off your expensive wedding gift," she said smiling. "That will be just fine, Mrs. Utley," Nan replied, not smiling "Excellent then!" Mrs. Utley said, as she continued her conversation telling Nan not to blame her if he appears to be a mystery to all of them including her! "No!" Nan replied. "He's not a mystery, Mrs. Utley. He is my husband Mr. Sturgis Winters," "Oh, well all of that may be true but you must admit, rushing off getting married in such a hurry in secret and all. What else do you expect people around here to think?" continued Mrs. Utley. Nan had no reply. She sat quietly. "Now come on Nan you can tell me I won't tell anyone." Mrs. Utley said seated next to Nan scooting closer, to her leaning her ear over near Nan's mouth trying to get her to whisper something that wasn't true. "Come on… You can tell me I won't breathe a word of this to anyone." Mrs. Utley assured Nan. "You can trust me. Now tell the truth… we won't be having any little Winters surprises running around here in a few months, will, we now?" Looking directly at Nan's husband, Sturgis, who sat patiently in silence until now he had taken as much as he could from Mrs. Utley's false innuendos about his wife's, virginity. He stood to his feet saying, "Mrs. Utley, to clear up any and all doubt or false rumors about my wife. Let me proudly be the first to tell you. My wife, Mrs. Nan Winters was pure and untouched when I met her. She was untouched and pure when we consummated our marriage. And I'm sure Mr. Utley, in all his modesty if he could remember that far back in time would say the same about you, on your wedding night." "Well…" She gasped. "Oh, my how courageous he is gallant, how noble and he comes on cue too! Now, now Mr. Winters. There's no need to get upset or display your chivalry. We're just having a little girl talk, that's all," Mrs. Utley said, smiling at the same time looking around the room for a maître de. Instead she sees Miss Ya'vett La' Cure with her new fiancé` Mr. Warren Lowell III. "Oh! Look! There's Miss La' Cure with Mr. Lowell…don't they make a dynastic couple? Destined for greatness, those two," While Mrs. Utley spoke she took her hand waving it, beckoning them to the Winters' table for a belated celebratory champagne toast to the newlyweds. Telling everyone at the table including those coming, "Don't worry, my husband will pick up all cost for this afternoon's luncheon so eat hardy, enjoy yourselves," When Ya'vett and Warren arrived at the table everyone introduced themselves. Mr. Utley came back over to join in on the toast, "Champagne for everyone!" proud with loud Mrs. Utley voiced.

Well into lunch. Warren announced that Ms. La' Cure had consented to marry him in the spring of next year. He proudly removed her glove showing off the engagement ring he chose for her. Informing all at the table that their cruise ship was scheduled to set sail in the morning. They were traveling abroad so his bride-to-be could meet the rest of the Lowell Family. "Oh! My! How wonderful! A spring garden wedding, I just love spring weddings, you know. Don't you love them Mrs. Winters?" she said looking at Nan. "They're so romantic, you know. Much better than running off getting married to some stranger in the dark. Oh, my I'm so excited! I can hardly wait I can hardly contain myself!! A lovely spring wedding," Mrs. Utley was more than glad, clapping her hands together, grinning, speaking, as her voiced reached higher than soprano range. "Oh, my what a wonderful wedding that will be and how wonderful it will be having in full bloom an entourage of gorgeous cascading flowers, to choose from like roses, pansies, golden daffodil with having so many, many more. "Aaah," Mrs. Utley expressed with gladness and excitement almost to the point of exhaustion as she took in a deep breath from jubilation, "And let's not forget the monarch butterflies, joining those little teeny tiny hummingbirds, flying all around fluttering their little wings. Adding, that special, wonderful, accented touch to any spring garden wedding. How exciting! And yes, like I always say… There's nothing like a beautiful spring wedding. I can hardly wait to attend!" she said standing to her feet with smiles of enthusiasm, "How wonderful this moment is! Now we have two congratulatory celebrations to toast this afternoon. "Now, before I forget let me ask are there anymore surprise announcements we should be toasting today. Mrs. Utley said looking at

Nan, smiling and Nan smiling, back. "None?" Mrs. Utley asked again, for confirmation. It was silent at the table.

Mrs. Utley took that opportunity to tapped her fork on the crystal water goblet that was resting on the table next to Mr. Utley she was keeping everyone's attention so that everyone would join in on the toast "Well... then glasses up!" she almost shouted. All and all the luncheon went wonderfully. With everyone talking, eating, drinking, laughing and celebrating no one thought to return to their own tables. They stayed at the Winters' table enjoying a delicious lunch, having a grand time with listening to more of Mr. Utley's hilarious martial jokes. This gave way to a memorable afternoon so much that no one had room for dessert except Mrs. Utley. Who ordered a triple layer chocolate cherry cheesecake topped with flaming mint cherries insisting that everyone stay until she finished, eating. And they did. Later, Mrs. Utley made an announcement promising to start her diet on Monday. "Oh... No, not again," Mr. Utley was overheard whispering to himself. "Not another broken diet promised." Sturgis smiled at Mr. Utley's funny comment about his wife's broken diet plans with promises and it was obvious. Still all who attendance said the luncheon was great!

Soon after, everyone began leaving the restaurant to board their carriages. Nan took a few minutes to stopped and talked with Ms. La Cure. Who promised earlier when she and Lowell returned from their trip she would stop by the gift shop to look at oil paintings they'd spoken about today at the luncheon. Nan shared with Ya'vett and Warren that she had several in stock mostly from local artists like Zines, Tas, Ni' and other fine artists in the area. She felt they would be pleased owning any paintings bought from her shop. And she looked forward to having them as happy returning patrons, soon. "Splendid! Ya'vett smiled further saying, "Mrs. Winters according to our travel itinerary we should be gone several months but I will keep you scripted regarding our return date," "Thank you, Miss La'Cure, that will be great!" Nan said shaking hands in a potential purchase agreement, sealing the deal. "Safe sailing to you both," The Winters said getting into their carriage. "Why, thank you," they replied as they boarded theirs.

Inside their carriage, Nan scooted close to her husband smiling, holding his hand as she whispered these words to him, "Sturgis dear, I hope their married life together will be as wonderful as ours," Sturgis didn't reply right away. He waited moments before expressing, "Well dear, I'm sure it will but one never knows," While he shared those words with Nan, his wife Sturgis sat close, to her smiling, too. And although their ride to the shop was short it was still romantic with the driver blushing on occasion from the sounds he heard from inside their moving carriage. When the Winters finally arrived they stepped out of their carriage, meeting Mr. Toliver not far from the shop door, he handed Nan the mail. "Here you go Mrs. and Mr. Winters. I must say these congrats are still coming in. That's wonderful! I'm glad for you two! But you know I haven't been feeling well, lately," "Oh really! Sorry to hear that Mr. Toliver," Nan said. "Yeah, I feel a little run down more than anything else. I may need to take some time off for rest with a little relaxation of course. I may even do some fishing," he stated. "Now, that would be nice," Sturgis added. "Yes and boy will my wife be glad when I do." He remarked. "I'm sure she will," Nan replied. "Yeah, I agree. I'm sure she will. Oh well, take care, see you tomorrow afternoon," Mr. Toliver said. "Yes, that will be fine, Mr. Toliver but only if you're up to it," the Winters replied. "Yes, I'm sure I will be and you two take care, as well, Oh, and da' I'll stop by as soon as I'm up to it I'd like to buy several new fishing poles. You know I've had my eye on one in particular for a long time, now. But I'll get back to ya'," He said walking slow down the walkway not having at all that bust of energy he was known for. Nan watched Mr. Toliver leave with concerns. She was just about to call out to him, when. "Oh! Mrs. Winters I'm so glad you're back!" Hilda said running up to Nan in a panic. "What's wrong, Hilda?" Nan with equal concerns asked. It seems Hilda was upset because supplies were getting low. "I don't know how I let this happen. It's never happened before. We're getting extremely low on supplies! The ones we use most. Our daily main staples," she expressed. "Is that right? Are you sure, Hilda? We can't be," Nan said hurrying into the gift shop needing to see what Hilda was talking about, Nan saw for herself the almost emptied storage bins, shelves and closets. She knew Hilda was right. They needed those supplies in order to keep the gift shop opened and running. Nan not wanting to further alarm Hilda remained calm responding softly by saying. "Let's me see Hilda. What about those emergency supplies in the tapestry room? I know for a fact I checked them last week I was sure it was stocked with plenty. Hilda, you do know the closet I'm speaking about, don't you? The room where we keep those large deep storage bins?" Nan inquired. "Yes, ma'am, I've already checked those places ma'am nothing in there. Well… what about the bins in the cellar or those other storage places we use? "I don't know how I let this happened," Hilda upset kept repeating. "Now, Hilda, don't worry yourself about this we can fix it," Nan replied, but Hilda was nervous, in a frenzy about her oversight. Hilda felt if someone didn't act fast she was sure they would run out of supplies with not having enough to accommodate the many customers who come into the shop every day. So she made a costly request. "Ma'am, I've looked everywhere for more supplies but there aren't any here. We've used them all. Now, I know what I'm about to asked of you is going to be a bit costly but with your permission. I would like to rush a reorder right now, right away! You may take the cost out of my wages until it is paid for because it was my sole responsibility to monitor all supplies we use daily at this counter and in this shop. I failed to do so," Nan was surprised to hear Hilda confessed or even suggests this sudden request. But she told Hilda not to worry about the extra cost, "Let's just get those supplies ordered and ordered now!" "Why of course, ma'am," Hilda quickly responded. She immediately stopped packing several small brass chevalets putting them down on the counter giving Nan her full attention. Nan went on to tell Hilda. "To be on the safe side let's order four months of supplies that should be enough to hold us for a while. And it's my understanding if we order now, we should get them in time before these run out. With that in mind, when this rush order does come in, Hilda please put the extras in our storage bins, closets and in other places as before. Also, Hilda I would like to say the daily responsibility of monitoring supplies should not solely rest on your shoulders alone. Starting today we will all keep a written log of supplies we use every day around this shop. When supply levels are almost approaching low. We will reorder. Okay? Nan announced. "Yes ma'am she said still looking somewhat worried. "Now, see there Hilda I told you we could fix this, did I?" Nan said smiling giving Hilda a big hug making her feel better. And she did. Nan also reassured Hilda with these words. "Hilda, don't ever work yourself up into a tizzy like that, again. Things like this sometimes happen besides we've all forget to do something we felt was important myself included. And to me it isn't worth getting all that upset about but what is worth importance's to me is you." she said, getting the worry off of Hilda by saying words of truth. Then Nan switched the subject at the same time adding a little humor into the conversation by asking "Now, how was things around here in my absence, barring this of course," laughing she said. Hilda laughed too assuring Nan she and Alex handled the shop business well, as usual. Excluding, that one small exception. Nan and Hilda both smiled, "That's good to hear. I know I can always depend on you or Alex," she said walking toward the front counter, relieved. Now that Nan was back working the counter Hilda left to go into the kitchen. She decided to help Alex in the next room with the inventory backlog before it got too late. But first Hilda needed to finish her hot cup of tea. She told Nan on the way into the kitchen "Mrs. Winters there's a fresh pot of hot tea on the stove for you and Mr. Winters. So help yourself." she said walking towards the kitchen bypassing the room next door. "If, you need my help just ring the buzzer." she shared with Nan. "Okay thank you Hilda," Nan replied, she was standing at the counter opening mail while Sturgis was seated in a chair next to her humming. Then he looked up at her smiled and said. "Mrs. Sturgis Winters. I love the sound of that name," Nan said the name again this time louder, smiling, reading it from off a piece of mail that was just delivered to her, today." "Mmmm Hmmm I do too!" Sturgis replied as Nan leaned over kissing her husband on the forehead. "A beautiful name for a beautiful wife," he commented. Nan looked at the stack of unopened mail sitting on the counter then she shared with her husband, "All from well-wishers," she replied, "I don't know when I'm going to find the time to answer all this congratulations mail," she shared with Sturgis. "Oh, don't worry dear, you'll find the time, you're smart and beautiful. You're my wife. That's one of the reasons why I married you," he answered. "Oh really, Sturgis dear now tell me this please what are the others," Laughing Nan inquired as she gently tickled her husband trying to get him to confess the other reasons, why. She then noticed a familiar handwriting on a piece of mail, telling her husband. "Oh, Sturgis dear look, this one is from Tessa. You remember. I told you about her. We grew up together. We were like sisters. She has such a beautiful penmanship. Why, I'd recognize her handwriting anywhere,' Nan said. "Oh, yes Nan dear I do remember you telling me about her. How nice for you to hear from her," he said. "Oh my goodness Sturgis, Tessa is going to have her first baby in a few months shame on her keeping it a secret to surprise everyone here in town that Tessa always full of surprises!" Nan was happy to share that wonderful news about her best friend's new baby arrival with her, husband Sturgis. "Well that's good to hear Nan great for your play sister and her husband," Sturgis replied, smiling as he spoke those words. At the same time he was thinking about him and Nan's first child together. His thoughts were, "What does it feel like to be a dad? What would I name the child if it were a boy or a girl? I wonder how Nan would feel about me after becoming the mother of my child." Sturgis was deep in thoughts when Nan interrupted her husband's private moment, by speaking. "You know dear Tessa's husband always wanted a large family." Oh," Sturgis said "I never knew that. Now that's one you've never mentioned to me before," he said, smiling but not at what Nan said but at the thought of being a dad. "Yes it's true and it seems as if they are well on their way in starting one. Oh, Sturgis just think, one day it will be my turn to have a baby, our first child," she said. "Yes, dear I know," He replied, with a big grin on his face. "And we will have lots of beautiful babies to love and enjoy," Sturgis happily replied. Hilda sat quietly in the kitchen sipping her hot cup of tea wearing a troubled look on her face. She heard Sturgis' meaningful remarks about he, and Nan's off springs. But Hilda also knew that, what Sturgis wanted, was impossible. So she continued sitting in silence not meaning to eavesdrop but to enjoy her cup of tea before going next door to help Alex with the inventory. But she needed to sweeten her tea a little so she quietly got up to get some honey off the kitchen table. When she saw a customer coming up the walkway then into the shop Nan greeted him. "Hello sir," She said. "How may I help you?" She asked as he walked through the door. "Why, yes, I'm in need of buttons. Large black and white buttons about a dozen each should be enough. Oh, and a small bottle of Rose Port," the customer requested, "What vintage?"

Nan asked. "The oldest you have in." "Alright sir, I'll go check the cellar first then the stock room. My husband will keep you company. Be right back," she said. Sturgis was seated behind the counter he wanting to appear friendly opened the conversation to the customer with. "Yes, I too enjoy drinking a good glass of chilled rose port," he told the man. "Indeed" the customer said further adding." Precisely, but with absolute it must be an old vintage, served at the right temperature to be pleasing or pleasurable or effective to one's pallet wouldn't you agree, sir?" the man sharply stated. "I totally agree. I too concur it must be served at the right temperature. But it must be served at the right time of day, too. In my opinion that is what's most important," Sturgis answered clearing is throat between words toying with the man, making small talk, idle conversation which resulted into a battle of words between the two of them." Near the close of their discussion the customer, too wanted to have the last word, stating. "Now see here! Yes, again I must say …there's nothing like the bouquet, aroma not to mention the exquisite taste of a good bottle of rose port to drink while enjoying life," He said but Sturgis was determined to have the last word. He answered then further added. "Indeed and I too say it must be served at the right time of day, too to be effective!" "Now, see here!" agitated, the customer almost shouted as he ended his conversation with Sturgis.

Nan soon returned with a dusty, cool, dark glass bottle in her hand. She was happy to have had the port in stock but sorry she didn't have any buttons for the customer. Nan showed him the bottle. He was very pleased. "That will be perfect," he said. Nan told the man she needed to rinse it off with cool water then wrap it for him, "Will news press or a different kind of wrapping paper be alright with you? I'm out of my regular wrapping paper. But it should be arriving any day now," she told the customer. "That will be just fine in fact I prefer news press it's a better insulator," he answered. "Well good then I'm pleased. It won't take me but a few minutes more," she told him. "And sir, if, you like there's a tailor shop, Wetzel's, about two streets over." She was sure he would find all the buttons there he needed. "Why, thank you very much, ma'am I'll stop by there on my way home," he replied counting his change holding it in his hand looking around the shop wanting possibly to make another purchase. He looked at a few more items in the shop. The customer walked by a display table he stopped picked up, held in his hands a pair of child sized wooden Dutch clogs. He looked at the beautiful hand painted red and yellow life-like tulips on the shoes thinking about his granddaughter, laughing a little remembering her first clumsy steps walking in a pair that looked just like these. He put them back onto the shelf, still smiling. Satisfied with what was already purchased. In his turn to leave the customer could not help in noticing what was mounted on the wall. "Magnificent," he whispered, stopping, almost dropping his change starring inside the glass case where Nan's seashell collection was housed. "Superb…how striking!" He almost shouted putting his package back down onto the counter and his change into his pocket, as he slowly walked toward the glass case, reaching out to touch it. "Amazing," he whispered gawking, gazing at the colorful wall mounted case. "Why… I've never see unusual colors like that before, colors beyond the rainbow," He pausing a moment before speaking again, softly said, "Is that yours?" he asked. "Yes," Nan proudly replied. "My… If only an artist brush could capture those brilliant hues on canvas. Now! That would be a priceless portrait!" he stated. Later asking Nan, if she ever thought about selling her collection of seashells?

And if so what price would she ask? Nan told the man her father started that "Mother of Pearl" collection for her when she was a little girl. It meant so much to her that she could never sale it to anyone, for any price. She'd had it all her life and to her that feeling too is priceless. The gentlemen smiled, picked up his package, tipped his hat bidding Nan and Sturgis a good, happy life together.

Minutes later, Hilda buzzed for Nan to come into the inventory room. She needed to ask Nan what to do with the box that had the words written on it "Throw Back into The Sea" Should she open it or did Nan want to open the box herself? Nan told Hilda, "Leave that one out. Place it on a shelf inside the wall tapestry room and I'll open it later," Alex was still seated at the table opening incoming merchandise he suddenly became uneasy at the sheer mention of that box. Wearing, a worried look on his face every time someone talked about it made him feel uncomfortable. He didn't like having it around. He always believed Nan should have thrown it back into the sea. His thinking was the day Nan found the box was the day she found the stranger. And having the box around was a constant reminder of that day…A day Alex was trying to forget. "I'm done for the day Ms. Hilda, please tell Mrs. Winters that I will see her tomorrow," Alex said. "Yes, Alex I sure would love to but you can tell her yourself. She's standing over there," Hilda replied. "Oh, is she" he said. "I didn't see her standing there. I must be a lot more tired than I thought." They all laughed. Well… Then see you tomorrow Mrs. Winters," he said. "Yes, dear, that's okay," Nan replied. As they gather up their stuff to leave Nan was picking up the inventory log-in-ledgers that were on the table, placing them on her desk. It was getting late, long passed closing time so she helped Alex and Hilda with their caps, coats and sweaters. Later she turned off all gift shop lights for the night. Nan watched through the shop window as they boarded the carriage. Hilda was headed for home. Alex was being dropped off at the orphanage. Along the way for some unknown reason to Hilda, Alex said. "You know Ms. Hilda, one day I'm gonna have a house of my own to live in with a successful business, too just like Nan's…I mean Mrs. Winters, just you wait and see," he shared. Hilda chuckled once and said as their carriage rode off. "Yes, Young Mr. Alex… I believe that to be true. I believe that to be true."

Tomorrow was Wednesday. The shop was closed. Nan and Sturgis slept late after a nightly stroll along the beach. But the strangest thing happened. It was somewhere between midnight and daybreak Sturgis Winters eyesight returned. It happened rather oddly. When he woke up the following morning he could see. Even he couldn't believe it. He wanted to be sure before telling anyone. So he, Sturgis quietly sat up on the side of the bed, rubbed his eyes, opened and closed them several times. Smiling pulling down on his face, blinking his eyes, he wanted to laugh out loud, but didn't. Instead he placed his hands over his mouth laughing quietly in them and to himself trying not to wake Nan. Sturgis decided to carefully stand to his feet he walked through the house, then the gift shop, picking up looking at items that were on the shelves. Afterward putting them back into place he touched and felt sea objects like a dry prickly star fish that rested on the counter. He stopped to touch and pick up a habergeon that was still packed inside an opened wooden crate sitting on the table. His mind went briefly back to the knight or knights that wore it, realizing how heavy it really is. Sturgis walked down aisles looking at merchandise inside of Nan's shop, amazed at her inventory. He then went into the kitchen following the aroma of Hilda's homemade apple cinnamon oatmeal raisin cookies. Finally, he sees what they look like stacked on top of each other inside a glass cookie jar, reaching in he took one. One bite then another "Mmmm," he whispered leaving the uneaten cookie resting on a plate near the sink. Sturgis was happy, excited about his returned sight. He went over to the kitchen curtains, took a peep out of the window then threw a kiss to the sun. For the first time Sturgis was looking at the place he had called home for such a long time. He was happy his sight returned. Wanting to share this good news with his wife he quietly got back into bed and scooted closed to Nan. Sturgis tried awaking her with morning kisses on the side of her face. Nan laid there on her stomach sleep with her long auburn hair covering the pillow. He gently brushing it backed, leaning over to give her a kiss speaking in a low voice, "Good morning, Good morning Mrs. Winters, Wake up. I have a surprise for you." Nan was always receptive to his desires she woke out of a deep sleep, raised her head pushing back her hair and slowly turned her face toward her husband. It was then he saw Nan's face for the first time. Immediately he yelled, screamed. "Ah! Ah! Ah!" kicking bed covers off his legs trying to get out of the bed grabbing his eyes, covering them. "What's the matter, dear?" Nan asked with loving, concern trying to comfort her husband. "What's wrong dear?" she softly asked in her gentle voice. But he couldn't answer. Not that Nan. He saw. He didn't know her. Sturgis didn't know what to do. She was a stranger to him. He had gotten used to and fell in love with Nan's voice. Not her face. The same voice he was hearing speak back to him did not match the face of gentleness, softness, purity and warmth. It was the welcoming speech of her voice which helped nurture him back to good health. Not the face of the person that was standing next to him. And he avoided looking at it. Covering, his eyes with his hands pretending to be having eye pains. "Hu," "Hu," "Hu," these eyes pains," he faked saying, "My eyes, my dark glasses. Get me my dark glasses!" he shouted as he stood trembling. He was quiet for a moment not knowing what else to say. Thinking? *"How can this be? When did? How could this have happened? To someone so loving, with such kindness, a gentle spirit and a heavenly voice to have such a horrid face, is unexplainable?"* He was dazed still in shock, in denial. Sturgis had to let what he just witnessed about his wife settle in. While still trying to cope, deal with the disbelief. Nan hurried to get dress telling Sturgis not to worry, giving him his dark glasses. She was going to get Dr. Laris. But Sturgis could not allow that to happen. He knew Doctor Laris would immediately know that his sight had returned. So he convinced Nan they were just eye pains he was having and for her not to worry because he gets them all the time. "Are you sure, you're alright, Sturgis, dear?" Nan asked, attempting to hold, kiss and comfort her husband through his painful ordeal. As she had done in the past with his prior accident and he was doing his best to avoid looking at her. "Yeah…I'm fine Sturgis said looking away, cringing," He later expressed, "Nan, dear I didn't want to alarm you but you see I still get these eye pains now and then I never wanted to bother you with it because they eventually go away. Nothing to worry yourself about Nan or get upset they come when they come. I just need to rest my eyes for a little while and they will go away. I've learned to deal with them," he told her. Nan was somewhat relieved after that statement coming from her husband but she told Sturgis, "If you have any more of these painful eye attacks I'm going to get Dr. Laris, no talking me out of it the next time!" she said sitting down. Then she got up walked towards the kitchen to pour them both a cup of hot coffee. Sturgis at that moment could have, but didn't, tell Nan that his eyesight returned. Instead, he was doing his best to avoid looking at her.

He finished drinking his hot cup of coffee. Staying in the bedroom most of the morning seated in a thick padded-arm, chair, still slightly trembling, wearing those dark glasses, pretending to be asleep, but really thinking serious about his wife's unsightly facial appearance. And most importantly he was thinking about what he was going to do now and how he was going to do it.

As the afternoon fast approached Nan went back to check on her husband, knocking on their bedroom door before entering the room. "Sturgis dear, how are you feeling, now?" Nan still concerned inquired. "Oh, ah, I'm feeling well, thanks for asking," he replied. "Well, then that's good to hear, Ah, Sturgis, dear now perhaps this might not be the best time to bring this matter up. So, please forgive me dear if it isn't. But earlier this morning you mentioned something about a surprise. What surprise dear?" Nan asked, waiting for an answer and with that statement she caught Sturgis totally off guard. He carefully searched for words while still remembering the disappointing surprise she gave him this morning. "Aaa! Surprise," he repeated. "Yes, dear a surprise," Nan softly answered. "Yeah," he said searching for words. "Theeaah, thee aah surprise, thee aah, theeeaaah, opera! That's it! That's what it was, the opera tonight!" He almost shouted walking towards Nan in fear while trying to smile. He was still wearing his dark glasses really heading to the other side of the bedroom away from Nan. Sturgis was pretending to be blind as he felt his way in the bedroom then as a romantic gesture he briefly took hold of her hands, in passing then carefully dropping, them. His sight was set on that small dark bottle of eye drops sitting on the nightstand. He needed that as the excuse to keep his distance from her but Nan always wanting to assist her husband in every way rushed toward the nightstand, too reaching for the bottle of eye drops, first. "Oh, I can get that for you dear I can put the drops in your eyes," she said almost grabbing the bottle. But he grabbed it up first saying, "No! That won't be necessary. I'm quite capable of doing this menial task all by myself. I don't need your help, that won't be necessary," Sturgis abruptly said, holding the bottle tightly in his hands looking at her in anger, feeling deceived. He was upset with Nan for not telling him what he found out about her this morning. Nan tried talking to him but not about her appearance. That subject didn't come up. Instead she offered him something to eat and another cup of coffee. He sharply told her, as he looked away, "No…I don't need or want anything, from you!" She later left the room feeling hurt, insulted by her husband's belittling remarks and his rude behavior towards her. Leaving him alone in the room to sit in silence having to cope with what he found out about his wife, giving this whole ordeal a great deal of thought. When suddenly it dawned on him, he had no money, no friends and no place to go. Sturgis had to be nice to Nan, regardless of or in spite of her unsightly appearance. So he decided to change his distancing mood, becoming more pleasant, loving, warm and inviting. He called Nan back into the room only this time in a soft, sweet, pleasing, beautiful tone. "Oh, Nan, Oh, Nan dearest could you please come here please, dear?" Nan slowly entered the room saying, "Yes, Sturgis the husband," she was, still bruised from his rude behavior, his lashing tongue. Sturgis smiled as he quickly stretched out his arms, opening his hands, reaching for her, grabbing, hold to her hands kissing them confessing, "I'd like to apologize for my insensitive outburst moments ago, it's those eye attacks. You know the ones I just told you about. They can be very painful at times and it seems as though I've passed my pain on over onto you. Please forgive me, Nan dearest I'm so sorry it will never ever happen again ever I promise. And to make up for my terrible display of ignorance's I still want to surprise you as I mentioned this morning. I would love to take you out tonight, if that's alright with you?" He expressed. Nan's unhappiness instantly blossomed into smiles of forgiveness, "Oh, Sturgis dear, yes that would be wonderfully fine. I would love to go out with you tonight. And yes, I do accept your apology I know you're not mean or grumpy. It was those ol' eye pains you had earlier this morning that caused you to act so rude towards me. I understand dear," smiling she said. "Good then, so, I'm forgiven?" he asked. "Oh, yes, dear, forever always I forgive you," she shared. "Sturgis was thrilled expressing, "Nan, dearest because I know you love going to the opera and I do too! I'm only sorry my sight hasn't returned I was hoping it would have by now I also realize I'm missing out on seeing the excitement of an opera with all that it brings those brilliant costume designs, exciting performances not forgetting the crowds of people, oh, my!" At this point in the conversation Sturgis lowers his voice to the tone of pity. "I also know it's no fun going with me, having to contend with a person of limited sight. But I'm willing to sacrifice my feelings and go, sit and listen, to the music of your world. As I sit beside you alone in my own dark world. Just as long as I can continue to go with you my wife, Mrs. Sturgis Winters in whom I am extremely proud of, if that's alright with you, Nan dearest," "Oh! Sturgis, that's so sweet of you, you're always thinking about my feelings, forgetting all about yours. You're so unselfish, dear." Nan was almost in tears to quickly reply, "As I have always assured you Sturgis don't worry, your sight will return soon. I'm sure of it," Nan expressed with happiness as she rushed to dress for the opera. And he, Sturgis left the room slowly whispering, to himself. "Yes, dear you're right. I'm sure it will."

Since the marriage of Nan to Sturgis, the gift shop was now closed on Wednesdays. Alex came on his off day to work helping Nan with inventory backlog along with other job related responsibilities. He started his workday off by opening, recording and stocking all new incoming merchandise from the sea, dock deliveries and trade items. But it was this unfinished game Alex and Nan needed for a victor that obviously upset Mr. Winters. Sturgis was seated in another room. He faintly overheard Nan and someone else's voice in the dining room. He listened to the sounds of laughter becoming even more curious then decided to go investigate. Waiting outside the door, he snooped, eavesdropped overhearing Nan and Alex who were having a good time playing chess. They were laughing, joking around. "Check Mate!" Nan shouted. "Oh! Nan! I mean Mrs. Winters. You've, won again! But that's okay I won twice last week, remember?" Alex happily said. "Yes, you sure did, Alex, but this is a new week and I won this game," she said laughing almost out of breath when in walked Sturgis. "I thought the boy was getting paid to work!" Sturgis said in a rough, deep tone, barging through the room, bumping into their table, knocking down green jade chess pieces off the board on purpose onto the floor. Nan and Alex flinched. She then did her best to appease her husband by gently voicing, "Yes, dear he is but you know I always play chess when we have the chance besides we needed to finish this game for a winner. Isn't that right Alex?" Nan looked at Alex, smiled and said.
But Alex was slow to say, "Yes, ma'am you're right. We always play when we get the chance," not smiling, he remarked. "Now, Sturgis we're just having a little fun that all before we start back to work. We won't work long today because I have a very important date tonight with my handsome husband. Who's taking me to dinner, isn't that right dear?" Nan said grabbing hold to Sturgis' hand pacifying him hoping that would help break some of the tension in the room. Then Sturgis gently pulled away feeling a little intimidated. It was strange to him seeing Alex for the very first time which made him realize Alex was no longer a boy, but was in the beginning of manhood. He looked at Alex through his dark glasses, having to come to terms with the fact that Alex would be a man soon and then what part would he play in Nan's life. Alex himself could feel the tension Mr. Winters brought into the room. He told Nan that he had better get back to work. "I'll be there in a moment, Alex. Are you still hungry?" Nan asked. "Yes, ma'am I am," he replied. "Okay young man I'll fix you a nice big sandwich along with

a glass of cold milk is that alright, with you?" she asked. "Yes…that will be just fine Nan." "What? What did you say, boy?" Sturgis sharply shouted. "I meant Mrs. Winters," he replied. Sturgis is fully aware of Nan and Alex's special bond. There is closeness between though two that even Hilda couldn't break. And Sturgis would be very foolish if he tried to tamper with it. They worked into the evening catching up on most of the backlog, both telling funny jokes, each trying to outdo the other, with Nan laughing at them all. Then she took in a deep breath, from being a little tired, expressing, "Well, Alex we're almost done. We can finish what's left on tomorrow if we have the time, remember I have a date tonight," smiling she said. "Oh yeah, that's right I almost forgot," Alex said. "Oh, well then see you tomorrow Mrs. Winters and dado have a grand evening," Alex said, leaving. "Why, thank you, young man," smiling Nan replied. And she did.

It was always hectic the next day after being closed. Nan kept watching for Alex to walk or run through the door on time. He didn't. He was late again. Hilda hadn't shown either. Instead her niece Abby came in her place telling Nan her Aunt Hilda was in bed down with the gout and she didn't know when she would be up or out of bed. Nan didn't have time to reason. She needed help. "Alright…Abby you can work in your aunt's place until she's well enough to return. Please inform her when you leave work today, alright," Nan told her. "Oh, yes ma'am," Abby said, smiling "I most certainly will Mrs. Winters, and thank you. The money will help us out, greatly," she replied. Abby had worked at the shop before when Nan and Sturgis were on their honeymoon so she was familiar with the shop duties. Sturgis was helping by keeping the ladies in conversation as Nan waited on customers, ringing up their orders and wrapped them, too. Abby went right to work putting on an apron assisting customers, when in walked, "I'm here to pick up my dwarf trees. The Yen, the Baobab and let's not forget my rare signature orchids. They've come all the way from the continent of Africa. They're rare you know, very rare. Are they still here?" Mrs. Utley inquired. "Oh, yes Mrs. Utley they're still here," answered Nan talking to her while waiting on other shoppers. "Good Afternoon, Mrs. Utley," Abby said seeing that Nan was overwhelmed helping other patrons. She also knew that Mrs. Utley was the kind of patron that did not like to wait for service. But rather be waited on and quickly too. "Good day, Abby," Mrs. Utley said, then she paused before speaking, looking at Abby taking a step back, "Oh, my… what a beautiful young woman you've become. I heard you were employed at this establishment, yet every time I stopped by to shop you weren't present. Oh, well, anyway you're here now, Abby it's good to see you again young lady and won't you please give your aunt my best will you, dear?" Mrs. Utley stated. "I sure will ma'am," Abby replied, smiling. Sturgis too heard those words about Abby's beauty, turning his sight in Mrs. Utley's direction.

Mrs. Utley was right. Abby was a pretty young woman. With hair, redder than the autumn leaves she was tall, lean, with a hand full of freckles, and a dazzling white smile. And her glowing personality only enhanced her beauty. Sturgis was enjoying the sheer sight of Abby letting his old man's imagination run young forgetting all about Nan, his wife. Abby was helping to assist Mrs. Utley by opening boxes, allowing her to inspect the dwarf trees along with rare orchids she had purchased earlier in the year assuring her that the merchandise was undamaged with a safe arrival. "Aren't they lovely? Mrs. Utley said. She further spoke. "You know... I am a collector of dwarf trees along with rare orchids. Oh my yes, just look at these! I have the perfect place for these rare beauties," she said grinning with delight. Until... she took a closer look. Mrs. Utley stopped abrupt right in the middle of her conversation with Abby. "Hey! Hold it! What is this? What's going on around here? Is someone trying to pull one over on me," She, noised discovering her signature orchids were root-rot. "These things are root-rot!" she screamed, adding, "I demand a full refund immediately! What do you people take me for an, idiot? Why, I've paid a great deal of money, months in advance for these rare orchids and I'm going to get to the bottom of this!" Nan heard Mrs. Utley's outcry but she was extremely busy. Nevertheless, Nan took the time to tell her, not to worry. That she could still take the orchids if she wanted at no charge to her, if it meant calming Mrs. Utley's nerves. She'd also had options for now or later to get a full refund or store trade credit. "Now that's more like it!" Mrs. Utley smiling shouted back at Nan over the noise inside the shop. Somewhat satisfied she told Abby to go ahead put the orchids, dwarf trees along with the other packages in her carriage, opting for store trade credit, she wanting to settle it now, shouting, "Right now! I demand immediate service, right now!" Nan was swamped with other customers. In her wait, Mrs. Utley glanced down at her watch remembering she had a women's meeting to attend. She suddenly changed her mind. Informing Nan, smiling. "I will return again on another beautiful day to complete my trade credit transaction. I can see you are overworked, too consumed with others. As you well know Mrs. Utley does not wait for services rendered. Or will I arrive late for my meeting, either. After all I am the keynote speaker, you know," Mrs. Utley felt if Nan had waited on her now she would not give her the strict personal attention. Mrs. Utley feels she is warranted. Besides it's no secret everyone in town knows when you're doing business with Mrs. Ethan Utley, be prepared to give all your attention because she will demand it. "And thank you, for coming in to shop with us today Mrs. Utley," Nan shouted, smiling as Mrs. Utley was leaving the gift shop.
"It's the black carriage with the large 24 karat gold "U" monogram on the doors. I thought you would have found it by now, young lady but I see you decided to be sure and wait for me. Well, done let's go dear," she told Abby. "Yes ma'am," Abby responded pushing a cart filled with merchandise, making her way down the walk to Mrs. Utley carriage. Alex too was on the walkway rushing passed, brushing too close to Mrs.

Utley, but spoke. "Good day Mrs. Utley. Sorry for the rush, I'm late for work," running right into the shop door. "Slow down young man before you cause injury to someone," she shouted. "Yes…ma'am. Sorry again," he shouted back at her. Nan told him she didn't have time to discuss the matter regarding his late arrival to work, they could talk later. "Let's wait on our customers," she said with a smile. Alex went into one of the gift shop's back rooms looking for his work vest, to put on. Sturgis followed him trying to be nonchalant with singing, "doe," "dee," "doe," "doe, doe," Sturgis hummed, feeling his way moseying toward Alex commenting," Ah…Hum. I, ah heard you were late, again," looking at Alex trying his best to intimidate him. Alex ignored Sturgis, not saying a word to him. That only made Sturgis react saying by saying, "Ah, they ah, they don't have clocks at the orphanage anymore?" He stood facing Alex with his arms folded, meddling. Alex stopped removing his jacket. He started to open his mouth to respond. Then he decided to close it further ignoring Sturgis, "What did you say boy, hu?" Sturgis said, further adding, "I thought I heard you say something?" Alex looked at Mr. Winters and smiled he found him rather amusing snickering once at him but kept his mouth closed. "Haaa you better not have…and don't be late again, you hear me?" Mr. Winters said, speaking in a low, stern, tone not wanting Nan to hear him and then shaking his finger in Alex's face. Alex eventually got tired of Sturgis bullying him and he finally opened his mouth and said. "Excuse me, sir but I don't see your name anywhere out front on this gift shop, sir. And da' hmm…I've always thought this was Mrs. Winter's gift shop, sir," Sturgis went into a furious rage, almost lunging at Alex wanting to grabbed him. Alex was very polite in his flawless remarks surrounding Nan's gift shop. But it still didn't matter to Sturgis he began shouting at Alex in a whisper, "Why, why…you little… you just wait," Alex smiled, as he left Sturgis, angry, standing in one of the rear inventory room. He had no time for Sturgis' foolishness he had hurry to start work. Alex knew the history behind Nan's gift shop. It once belonged to Nan's father who started the gift shop for Nan when she was a child he then left it to her, his only daughter. Those true remarks made by Alex didn't sit well with Sturgis. They stayed on his mind all day into the evening, but he had a plan.

Later that night when he and Nan had retired for the evening Sturgis tried convincing Nan to replace Hilda with Abby, stating years of loyal service to her and the gift shop with the repeated task of carrying heavy packages from the beach to the wagon, up to the attic, down cellar steps and out to the barn, had finally taken its toll on the ol' girl. And that Nan shouldn't want to add any more pain or injury to Hilda's already aging body. "Oh, you are right dear but I don't know, Sturgis. Hilda is so much like family. I don't know, about that right, now," Nan replied. "What do you mean you don't know right now? If not now, then when? When will you know?" Sturgis demanded. Nan had no immediate answer for her husband so she remained quiet and still in the bed. "Well,

Nan at least give, it some serious thought. After all I should have some say in matters around here, don't you think?" Sturgis voiced, at the same time pulling the bed covers over his head. Turning his back to Nan knowing he had his own personal motives that involved Abby and not Hilda's wellbeing as he tried to portray. Sturgis felt if, he could replace Hilda with Abby that in time he could eventually replace Alex with someone else. Then Sturgis would have full control over the gift shop. On the 8th day of the month, tax bulletins were placed on all business owner doors in the area, including the gift shop, informing them of a tax increase to their property in ninety days. Abby stepped outside to get the posted bulletin for Mrs. Winters' and Alex on their return. Mr. Winters was somewhere in the shop or in one of the rear storage rooms. Abby stayed clear of him. It was something about him she did not trust. One reason was she always felt he could see but she dared not say anything to anyone in the shop about it. She didn't want to start a terrible rumor that may not be true. In doing so she would be jeopardizing her chances of keeping a job and destroying her Aunt Hilda's long-time relationship with Nan. Sturgis faked his blindness well. Like the time, Abby suddenly entered a room catching Sturgis reading a newspaper, startling him. He then pretended to be using it as a hand fan. Another time it was on a payday. Nan left Abby at the shop with Sturgis while she and Alex made a dock run, picking up other merchandise along the way. When Abby got home that evening she opened her pay envelope inside was extra money she did not work for, so she brought it back the next day which was her off day and to the attention of Mrs. Winters. Nan was busy helping customers. She stopped for a moment to hear Abby's concerns after hearing them she replied." Now, Abby…how did that much get in there? I don't remember putting that amount in there. But as you can see dear, Mrs. Winters is in a hurry I have to make another dock run," Nan expressed, she was fatigued taking in a deep then breath letting it out. "Oh! Well, Abby …because of your honesty and I know you need the money you may keep it, dear. Now as you can see Abby, I am extremely busy. I have to run an errand for this customer, too, but I'll be right back. If you like you may wait here for me to return so we can further discuss this matter. Or you may put on an apron to help out if you like or you may take the money with you and enjoy your day off," exhausted, Nan said, trying her best to smile. Sturgis was always present, listening. Abby felt, Mr. Winters put the extra money inside her envelope but she had no proof. It also bothered her when they were alone. Sturgis would speak exceptionally nice and sweet to her. He enjoyed saying, "Abby, sweet Abby. What can I get for my special girl, Abby?" He'd then wait for Abby to answer. Abby would always keep silent, working, thinking. *I'm tired of him saying this to me, he only says these words when Mrs. Winter and Alex aren't around. "If we didn't need this money…I'd walked right out of this shop and never come back!"* Abby would whisper that to herself but the truth was they needed the funds and Sturgis knew it.

The following Monday Dr. Laris came into the gift shop to return some cuff links he bought, but did not like the design. He told Sturgis he needed to come into his office for an eye examine soon. He also told Abby he had a message from her Aunt Hilda. "Tell my niece, Dr. Laris, said, I can return to work. I will be there in a few days." "Yes!" Abby almost shouted then smiled. Standing at the counter Sturgis heard Dr. Laris news to Abby from her Aunt Hilda. He was unhappy hearing the news about Abby leaving. So later that night at the dinner table he tried again to persuaded Nan to replace Hilda with Abby. "Not, just yet, dear. I don't think, now is a good time. We'll talk about it some other time, dear," Nan replied, giving her husband that excuse for the reason, why. Sturgis did not like that answer. He looked at Nan as she sat across the dinner table from him eating enjoying her dessert. His deep thoughts about her were, " *'How dare she, Why, that,'* " he whispered in disgust clutching his hand into a fist, holding it tight underneath the dinner table, releasing it. He quietly got up from the table leaving the room going into the kitchen and out of Nan's sight. Sturgis grabbed up a glass that was sitting on the sink, he held it high into the air, and squeezed it hard, crushing it in his hand without cutting himself. Venting feeling relieved as he walked down the hall feeling his way into the bedroom. Of course, he didn't sleep well that night having other things on his mind. And the time finally came. It was Abby's last day working at the gift shop. She was so happy for two reasons. One she'd found another part time job not far from the gift shop, which meant her aunt and she could still share the same carriage to and from work. It was her way of keeping an eye on Aunt Hilda's health without her knowing it. The other was Hilda is coming back tomorrow! "She'll be moving slow but she's coming back," And everyone was so glad! Well…almost everyone. Alex and Nan bought Abby "Thank you gifts" for working in her aunt's place. They hugged Abby. Wishing her well, further, telling her they would miss her but the good thing was her new job wasn't far from the gift shop. So she could keep in touch. Abby smiled thanking all of them as she went into the next room to put on her sweater to leave. She reached into her pocket for the carriage fare. Inside was a gold heart shaped locket. "Hmmm," she thought in puzzlement pulling it out holding it in the air looking at it as the gold locket dangled around the chain. She then held the locket inside her hand starring down at it, wonder who. Abby raised her head to look around still wondering… Who? And there standing in back of her starring from behind those dark glasses smiling was Sturgis Winters. It frightened Abby. She yelled. "Ooh, Mrs. Winters! Oh…Mrs. Winters! Mrs. Winters! I'm leaving now!" Throwing the locket down to the floor rushing out of the gift shop's back door slamming it! Sturgis found Abby's reactions extremely funny. He gave out a deep bellowing laugh as he reached down to pick up the locket. Tossing it into the air, catching it putting the locket into his pocket laughing again as he made his way into the kitchen for another slice of Abby's surprise "Thank you" cake.

The weather was nice when Hilda retuned to work. She was glad to be back moving a little slow, but glad to be back. She knew all the things Mr. Winters tried with her niece. Abby eventually told her aunt in confidence. Hilda didn't tell Mrs. Winters what she was told by her niece. She didn't tell anyone keeping it to herself for when the time was right. Hilda also noticed Mr. Winter's extreme rudeness his abrasive conversation toward Alex. Sturgis loved keeping a rift going between the two of them. He found fault or blatantly disagreed with just about almost everything Alex said or did. And she knew why…it was about dominance and control! An old jealous man's ego verses a young man's ego for dominance. Hilda didn't get involved. She merely observed hoping things would settle down between Mr. Winters and Alex. She, like Nan, would always be there for Alex if he needed her. By not letting Alex know was their way of making him a stronger, wiser young man with the ability to think and deal with whatever life or life's decisions are throws his way. Hilda's thinking was… *"Alex is a young man now. This is one of many life's fights he'll have to take on and win!"* Later, that afternoon a postman left a special delivery letter for Nan at the shop. *"Come quickly Nan! It's Tessa! The baby is breeched! Hurry, Trent."* Those are the words Nan read out loud to Sturgis in a letter from Trent, Tessa's husband. Nan prepared to leave immediately, but before leaving, she told Hilda, Alex and Sturgis, "I don't know exactly how long I would be gone. But I still have every ounce of confidence in all of you that you will run the shop well, while I am gone. And Sturgis, dear you are under the loving care and supervision of Hilda and Alex. They will make all the decisions regarding the shop. If extra help is needed there's always Abby." Nan said. Hilda smiled when Abby's name was mentioned. She hugged Nan, wishing her, Tessa and the baby "Prayers of Safety." "Oh! Alex," Nan said. "And don't forget to make the money deposits every Tuesday as usual," reminding him, before she left on her emergency trip to Tessa's home. "I won't forget, ma'am," Alex replied, helping Mrs. Winters' with her luggage, walking her to the carriage. I'll remember every Tuesday," Alex, repeated back to Nan, waving, goodbye, watching her carriage depart.

The running of Nan's gift shop went great, days passed quickly as customers came in and out shopping all day asking, *"Where's Mrs. Winters?" "When is she coming back?" "How's, Tessa and the baby?"* Hilda, Alex along with Sturgis answered all their questions of concern but by the end of the day Hilda said, almost laughing. "My!" Taking in a deep breath then letting it out. "This has been another long day. I'm pooped from working and answering so many questions! I'll be glad when Mrs. Winters return," Hilda wanted to take off her shoes to rest her tired feet but… "Oh wait! There's, my carriage! Let me grab my stuff. Oh, no! Look at those street beggars! When are they really going to stop them from bothering our customers?" "Wait Ms. Hilda. Don't worry about them… I'll walk you to your ride," replied Alex. "Why, thanks Alex. See you in the morning Mr. Winters…Oh, I left everything out you'll need for tonight on yours and Mrs. Winters bed, as I always do, dinner is already for you plated on the stove nice n' hot and I'll see you in the morning. Oh... and da' Mr. Winters I think I'll change things up a bit, how about I make you for tomorrow's breakfast a nice, fat, delicious pule cheese omelet with red potatoes and all the trimming. And I'll even bring a couple jars of my delicious plum preserves," she added. "Wow! Hilda, now that will be wonderful, just great!" Sturgis said with a big smile on his face going into a back room near the kitchen.

Once outside the shop, Hilda pulled Alex over to the side. "I need to talk with you. Walk close to me!" She whispered walking to her carriage. "Ms. Hilda has had a chance to observe lots of things that are going on around the shop. Some are fair. Some aren't. And so it is that way in life. But Alex, dear in this real world in which we live, people in it aren't always fair to us as we see it. They don't always talk, think, act or behave in a manner toward us like we would want them to. But put blinders on to them and you keep living, moving forward, doing what is right. Fix your eyes on yourself, your goals in life. And Ms. Hilda promise you will do well in this world... You will soar, you will excel in it. I promise. Now mind your manners. And Alex," Hilda whispered. "Yes, ma'am," he replied. "I want you to know Ms. Hilda isn't blind and I can hear pretty well too." "Yes, Ms. Hilda yes, ma'am!" he happily said running back to lock the shop door. When there was Mr. Toliver coming back, ringing the shop bell, with mail in his hands. "Oh! Alex! Great! Glad you're still here, thanks for letting me in!" Mr. Toliver was out of breath from rushing to the gift shop before it, closed. "I was just about to end my shift when I looked down into my bag I saw this package under some mail at the bottom of my mailbag." Mr. Toliver knew that Alex had been waiting for a while on this important package. "Sorry, I forgot to deliver this box when I came this morning. It must have gotten mixed-up in the mail. But any way here it is." "Oh! Boy!" Alex said with excitement, "My special model airplane set. Wow! It's finally here. Thanks Mr. Toliver. I've been waiting on this to come for long time. I can hardly wait to open it!" he said. Mr. Toliver smiled, handing Alex the slip for him to sign. He waited to collect the postage due. He told Alex before he could open the package he had to pay money for the postage that was due. "How much is it?" Alex asked looking at the price printed on the slip... "Oh! That much! Huh?" Alex was going through his pockets pulling out what money he had. Putting it on the counter, realizing he did not have enough. "Well...if you don't have enough I can take it back and bring it when you do. But remember I can only keep it a few days before I send it back, okay Alex? Seeing, Alex disappointed Mr. Toliver said, "Okay, I'll tell you what Alex. What if I bring it back tomorrow? Will that be enough time for you?" Mr. Toliver asked. "Tomorrow... Huh? Alex paused. Thinking not before speaking, he quickly said. "No... Wait! ... Mr. Toliver!" Alex badly wanted his model plane set. He had waited so long for and he wasn't going to let that plane set leave the shop without him having it. So he went over to the cashier drawer he reached in, got out money, handing it over to Mr. Toliver. Alex then reached for his package. Seated in the dark, watching from the other room was Sturgis. He witnessed that night Alex stealing money, from the cash drawer, seeing the entire illegal transaction. Sturgis could have at that time but didn't say anything to stop young Alex from stealing the money. It bothered Mr. Toliver too seeing young Alex take money from the cash drawer but he didn't say anything either. So that evening after leaving the shop Mr. Toliver kept quiet a little longer about it to Alex, allowing weeks to go by. He needed more time to ponder on what approach to take on how discussing with Alex about that night of his illegal financial transaction.

Early the next day Fritz came to the shop showing off his new bike. Alex had his new airplane set, doing his best to compete with Fritz's new bike, but to no avail. They loved taking turns riding the bike. The kids loved Fritz's new bike over new Alex's airplane set… Hilda watched though the front window. She could see the disappointment on Alex's face. Sturgis himself watched but from another shop window. He could see Alex's face filled with embarrassment from being ignored, seeing all the attention with excitement focused around Fritz's new bike. Alex felt the rejection hard. He tried to compete but no one was giving him or his air plane set any attention. So he decided to slip away from the small crowd without being seen. Embarrassed by the lack of attention that was given him with knowing those inside saw from the shop window, all the attention given to Fritz and his new bike, made Alex feel even worse. So he tried to enter into the back door unnoticed but was met by Sturgis who was blocking the door, preventing Alex from further entering the shop. Standing with his arms folded, peering down at Alex, having a grimace look on his face, Sturgis said, "Can't get by… huh?" Alex took a deep breath in and let it out. Then he politely said. "Excuse me sir." But Sturgis wouldn't budge. "Excuse me sir, I need to get through, sir." Alex said in a courteous tone. Sturgis still refused to move out of his way. He needed to go into the next room to put away his airplane set. Sturgis looked at the airplane set Alex was holding in his hands. He laughed then said, "Well…if you need to get through that badly, why don't you crawl into that little airplane of yours and fly over me," Alex waited a few minutes to reply then said. "Excuse me sir, but any idiot knows that's impossible.

Perhaps you haven't been informed of that, yet sir," Alex replied. "Why! You little…" Sturgis whispered not wanting Hilda to hear him, but still blocking Alex. When… "Alex I need your help, please! I can't open this box." Hilda shouted. "Yes, ma'am, right away," He yelled, smiling knowing Sturgis heard Hilda's request for his help, too. Sturgis had no other choice but to move out of Alex's way. So he could go to help assist Hilda. It was eight big boxes that Hilda couldn't open. They were filled with wrapping ribbon, twine, scissors, wrapping paper and other shop supplies. "Oh, my they've gone and changed the color of their mailing boxes again. No, wonder I didn't recognize them," she said. "Why'd they go do something like that Ms. Hilda?" curious Alex asked. "Oh, who knows Alex? Probably …to confuse me, I guess," Hilda answered, joking with Alex as he stood laughing opening the boxes for her. Business was very slow that day with only two customers coming into the shop all morning. It was now after twelve noon. "They all came yesterday spent their money," Hilda remarked quickly finishing up her snack. She needed to hurry rearrange old merchandise with new mixing them together and placing them on display tables for a quick sell. Alex was still taking supplies out of boxes putting them on the counter, saying, "Cheer up Mrs. Hilda, remember when I was little. You told me there would be some days in the shop we'll be so busy trying to wait on customers we'd be bumping into each other, almost falling down knocking ourselves out. And on other days we'd be falling asleep from the lack thereof. Remember saying that to me?" Alex asked. "Yes, Alex I do remember," Hilda said. "Well aren't these one of the lack thereof days?" laughing he said. "Why, yes, Alex. I guess it is," chuckling she replied. "But I'm just making lite of a gloomy situation that's all." They both laughed as Hilda took a big bite out of her freshly baked apple cinnamon raisin cookie. She turned it to Alex for him to take a big bite too, when Mr. Toliver surprised them both by walking through the door wearing a serious, but friendly look on his face. *"That's odd," Hilda whispered, "Mr. Toliver is not in his uniform and he took off work today. Hum, I wonder why?"* Mr. Toliver came by the shop to talk with Alex asking Hilda if it was okay to speak with him for a moment? She told him of course because business was real slow, today. Asking him, "Is it anything she could help him with?" Mr. Toliver replied, "Things are just fine Hilda but thanks for asking." He then told Alex that they should go out near the barn to talk. "You want to talk to me?" surprised, Alex asked. "Yes, Alex as a matter of fact I do," smiling, Mr. Toliver replied, "Okay, then let's go," Alex responded. When they got near the barn he told Alex the reason for this special visit from him was because of the money transaction a few weeks ago, "that postage due package" "Do you remember that night/" Mr. Toliver inquired. "Oh yeah, that, night, yes, sir, I do," Alex replied. "Good!" Mr. Toliver said. "Well it's because of that night I am here." He told Alex it bothered him that night to see him go into the cash drawer and get money out without letting anyone know or signing a cash removal slip showing where the money went. He then asked Alex did he sign such a slip. Alex told him, no. He asked Alex did he tell anyone he had taken or borrowed the money from the cash drawer. Alex told him "No, sir, I did not," "Why?" Mr. Toliver asked. "Well, I don't know why. I guess I am waiting on Mrs. Winters to return. Then I guess I would have told her." "Hum, I see," Mr. Toliver sighed. "Alex… Do you know the difference between right and wrong?" he asked. "Yes, sir I do," Alex replied. Mr. Toliver was glad to hear that response from Alex, he further said. "Well, that's great to hear, Alex!" He asked Alex the way he went about getting the money to pay for the airplane set, was it honest or dishonest? "Well," Alex said, taking a few minutes to think about his answer.

"Well…if you look at it that way…it looks as if it was dishonest." Mr. Tolvier was happy with that reply saying, "Well, said!" Mr. Toliver smiled, further saying, "Great answer, Alex!" and he gave Alex a hug. "Hey, why'd you go and do something like that, sir?" Alex asked. "Because you're a man of good conscience," stated Mr. Toliver. "A man of what?" Alex asked. "Well, Alex you may not understand what I am saying right now. But in time all of this will make good sense, to you. Always remember that and this, Alex, *Be a man in good standing. Be of good conscience. Do that which is right. Be honest. Show integrity and that integrity will preserve mankind.* Remember to do that, promise me Alex, you will," Mr. Toliver requested. "I will. I promise," Alex replied. "Good! That's what I want to hear you say, young man," pleased with Alex's answers Mr. Toliver left from outback of the shop happy heading for home.

It seems the novelty of Fritz's bike hadn't worn off. It was still popular with kids near the gift shop, especially those in the orphanage. The same orphanage Fritz was adopted from by an aristocrat family that made their money in tobacco. Even Penny was seen this time admiring Fritz's fancy clothes and riding on his new expensive bike. Alex could see all of this from across the street. Fritz with his ritzy lifestyle was still able to gather little crowds when coming down off the bluffs to visit. Telling the kids his father got him the most expensive bike Mr. Ingram had in his shop. And that Mr. Ingram has plenty of bikes but he got the best, the fastest and the most expensive bike in the shop. Alex was outside sweeping the gift shop walkway at the time Fritz was making his loud announcement. Looking over across the street at Alex, hoping he heard him, and he did. *"Aah! His fancy clothes and new bike ain't all that special. He always gotta come around here showing off, when he gets new things all the time,"* Alex said thinking to himself but speaking out loud, "Who are you talking to Alex?" Penny said, coming from across the street. "Oh, it's you. I didn't see you come up, Penny." Alex replied. "Hey Alex… I was gonna come over earlier, but the kids asked me to stay ride a little longer on Fritz's ol' bike. But you were right, Alex it ain't all that special. I really didn't enjoy riding it. I only rode on his new bike because everyone else rode on it." Penny stated, agreeing with Alex. Coming up the walkway overhearing his true comment about Fritz and his new bike, she further added, "Yeah… I road on his old bike and you were right again. It wasn't all that great." Alex didn't respond to Penny's comment right away. He waited before speaking. He stopped sweeping turned himself to look at Penny smiled then said, "Is that right?" Adding, "Now Penny it's hard for me to believe that statement coming from your mouth. Because every time I looked over across the street you were the only one yelling the loudest, wearing the biggest smile on your face riding on his new bike. And you rode three more times than any other kid over there. So don't try to sell me that malarkey!" Penny quickly changed the subject. She told Alex he left out of the orphanage this morning in such a hurry that he forgot to take the list for Ms. Hudgemen, one of the orphanage directors. So she sent Penny over with it to give to Alex. "Hey Alex, Mrs. Hudgemen would like to know if you have those items listed, in the shop?" she asked. "Well, Penny I don't know off hand. I'd have to go inside and see," Alex said, opening the shop door for Penny to enter with him following her inside. "Well, Alex what do you want me to tell her?" Penny asked. "Tell Ms. Hudgemen I will check our stock room later this evening. Then I will let her know for sure tonight when I get back to the orphanage." "Okay, Alex," she said in a hurry. Alex could see Penny glancing out of the shop window looking across the street at Fritz. He sensing that and not wanting her to get involved with Fritz decided, to use stalled tactics, by asking her rhetorical questions keeping her there with him in hopes that Fritz would get tired of waiting then eventually ride off. Alex started off by saying, "Hey! Penny you want to see me balance this broom on the back of my hand I bet you can't do this…see Penny." She watched for a few minutes moving closer to the door. "Yeah… that's nice Alex… Well I bet…" Alex knew Penny was ready to leave. He shouted her name out again getting her attention. "Hey! Penny! Where's, two cents?" Penny was at the door about to leave, but stopped to answer Alex's question. "Oh! That old dog! He just left. You saw him leave, Alex, you know he went to go chase Mr. Meeks' cat again," "Oh, yeah…that's right," Alex slowly replied. "Well, Alex, I… Au…Gotta. "Penny!" He shouted her name louder this time in desperation then brought his voice back to normal tone. Alex tried his best to keep Penny inside the shop with him and away from Fritz. "Hey I'll tell you what? Let's play a game of mumble-peg. I'll let you go first?" he said. With enthusiasm trying to make the game sound like real fun, more fun than riding on Fritz's new bike. "What, Alex? You want to play now, right now?" Penny stated, she was surprised he would ask to play that game, adding, "Wait a minute, Alex, now you know Hilda told us not to play that game anymore because it was too dangerous. Beside it takes too long to play that game you know all of this stuff anyway. What's wrong with you Alex why are you acting like this?" She asked. Alex had no reply. Oh, well Alex anyway I have to go. I'll see you later. I'll see you tonight, Alex. Bye," she said. Hurrying out of the shop rushing out the door almost catching her sweater pocket on the door knob Penny really didn't want to leave or hurt Alex's feelings. So once outside she stood in the middle of the street looking back at Alex inside the shop she waved then smiled. But headed to the small crowd that gathered around Fritz's bike sadly there was nothing Alex could do except look through the shop window in disappointment as he watched his friends appeared to be having a good time laughing, giggling smiling while riding on that new bike.

Ingram's bike shop wasn't far from the orphanage. So Alex decided to go by there on his way from work, already knowing he could not afford

any of those bikes but had a determined need to outdo Fritz. He just
wanted to take a look at them anyway. He was thinking ahead in case
Fritz asked him, "Where's your new bike Alex?" He could say, *"Yeah...
I went by Ingram's I rode on a few but I haven't made up my mind on
which one I'm going to buy."* Alex had gotten tired of being belittled by
Fritz's money and his rich lifestyle. He made up his mind that he was
not going to be embarrassed twice in front of Penny or his friends, again.
That same evening on Hilda's way home she made a stop at Eshman
Bakery she saw Alex. He was next door inside the bike shop sitting on a
new bike. She waited a few days to see if Alex would mention he had
stopped by there, but he didn't. So, she brought it up in her own subtle
way. "Alex, please help the customer with her packages would you
please, she needs your help," Hilda said. "Oh, yes excuse ma'am and
thank you for the tip," Alex said. Hilda decided this would be the perfect
time to use a little psychology on Alex to see if he would admit that he
was at Ingram's bikes. "My, that was a nice tip, Alex. If you keep
getting tips like that you'll be able to buy that new bike you've always
wanted at Ingram's," Hilda told him. Alex still didn't mention that he
was at Ingram's. Hilda patiently waited for him to bring up Ingram's on
his own or the fact that he was even there, but he didn't. He did however
comment. "Oh, yeah, ma'am, it would be real nice to have a new bike,"
he said, setting up stacking hand cranked Court Jester's-In-the Box
along with Colorful Marionettes putting them on a display table inside
the shop. Hilda then realized she was not going to get the answer from
Alex she was waiting for. So she turned her focus onto the display table
he was arranging. Telling him "those items will sell nicely," Hilda
reasoned with, the fact that he will tell her about Ingram's when he felt
the time was right.

Sturgis coming from the inventory room overheard their conversation,
he added in by stating "Like Fritz I suppose, next, you'll want to be
wearing those funny looking little new clothes like he wears and run
around here trying to talk like him too, I suppose!" "Mr. Winters...
Please!" Hilda pleaded, further saying, "Why... I think every young man
Alex's age should have new clothes to wear don't you think so, sir?"
Sturgis had no comment he just responded to Hilda's statement in
disagreement by sitting down near the counter's end putting a smirk on
his face pretending to be cleaning his fingernails. Hilda then told Alex,
"Keep working, saving your money and you'll have those nice things to
enjoy because you worked honestly for them," "Oh! My stars! What
time is it? I have to go pick up my husband's sea coat from the tailor. I
hope it's ready this time, because if it isn't? This will be my second trip
stopping by that tailor shop. It should be ready by now. Be back in a
bit!" "And, Alex, if I'm not back you can close up but I should be right
back," "Yes, ma'am," he replied. Alex saw Fritz coming up the
walkway with his new bike. Hilda meeting Fritz at the door, said.
"Well... hello Mr. young Fritz. My, that's sure a nice bike you have
there." "Why thank you! Ms. Hilda," he replied passing Hilda inside the

door, entering the shop. "Alex," Fritz speaking first to Alex as he walked toward jewelry inside the glass counter. "Fritz," Alex replied. Fritz added in his conversation, "I would like to buy something special for a special someone," He requested, looking down at the sparkling jewelry inside the glass case. Alex was hoping Fritz wasn't buying anything from that end of the glass counter, because every item in there was too expensive. He knew he could not match any gift inside the glass case if it were for Penny. "How much is this gold bracelet?" Fritz inquired, looking at a, gold bracelets lying on the black felt tray. "The price is tagged on the merchandise," Alex replied, watching him in envy, as Fritz was ready to make his expensive purchase. "I think this one is the best looking. However, it might be too large for her wrist. Do you size?" he asked. "No! You will have to take it to the blacksmith for that," Alex told him. "I see, well then give me a few more minutes to think about buying this piece of jewelry. I like it and I think she will too, but I don't have time to have it sized. I need to buy something quick but a gift that will please her something she'll enjoy, as well," he stated. Sturgis hearing them talk, added his remarks, "Is this someone special like a family member?" Sturgis asked, seated at the counter's resuming his pretend fingernail cleaning. "NO!" Fritz replied. "Is it a female? Huh?" Sturgis asked. "But of course," Fritz answered. "And Fritz if you don't mind me asking what age category are we talking about?" Sturgis asked. Then looked at Alex, knowing Fritz had to be making reference to Penny. "No, sir, I don't mind you asking. …She's about my age," Fritz told them. Sturgis found himself asking Fritz more questions. He wanted Alex to know that Fritz could strongly be talking about Penny. "Is…hum, she expecting this gift or will it be a surprise?" Fritz didn't answer that question, right away. He was pretending to be looking at other gifts. Then Fritz finally said. "It will be a surprise!" Alex was relieved. Sturgis intervened by saying "Well then, if she's not expecting it why don't you get something out of the purchase too? What about a nice box of chocolate candy? In getting that she will enjoy eating the chocolate candy and you can enjoy some too!" Fritz not answering right away ponders the suggestion then said. "That sounds reasonable enough. "I'm ready to place my order now I'll take four boxes, gift wrapped with large pink bows!" He requested. Alex started to wrap the boxes of chocolates. He tried not to listen too much into their conversation. Which might possibly involve Penny.

Alex wanted Fritz out of the shop. Fast. So he suggested. "Fritz would you like your order conveniently delivered? We do offer delivery service to our good customers," Alex said, "Oh no, my good man that won't be necessary I'll wait for my order, if you don't mind," Fritz replied. When that suggestion didn't work for Alex he tried to hurry with the wrapping of the boxes of chocolates. To expedite Fritz along but Sturgis had a few more questions for Fritz to answer, all the time watching Alex's facial expressions. Then suddenly Sturgis blurred out loud, "Yep! You can learn a lot about a man just by looking at his facial expressions, Yep, you can," he said, cleaning his fingernails. "Now, young Mr. Fritz is this special box of chocolate candy for you and your girl or will someone else be there too?" Sturgis inquired, knowing their conversation could quite possibly be about Penny. And that was personal to Alex. You could see Sturgis' words were getting next to him but he kept a straight face, concentrating on his gift wrapping of the packages. Alex hands wanted to shake from the pressure of Sturgis but he wouldn't let them, "No, sir, just she and I and again sir, she's not my girl just yet," Fritz was smiling as he answered Sturgis. Alex stopped wrapping the gifts, looking up somewhat relieved. He even smiled a little, to himself. Sturgis informed Fritz "Keep an eye on your bike outside. There has been a lot of theft in the area." "Probably those street beggars," Fritz said. "Or probably not," Alex answered looking Fritz straight in to the eyes. Fritz quickly looked out of the shop window keeping an eye on his new bike. "Well maybe you're both right," Sturgis remarked. Alex finished wrapping the boxes of candy then he asked Fritz. "Now, how are you going to pay for this purchase?" "Oh, but cash of course," Fritz answered. "Alex, you idiot!" Sturgis shouted standing to his feet. "What other way do you think he's to pay for his purchase. Why young Mr. Fritz here is a man of great wealth, not a penniless pauper. So remember that!" Sturgis sharply shouted. Alex had a strong comeback of words for Sturgis. "I have to ask these questions. He may have had trade credit to use, sir, but was unaware it was on the books, and if you remember correctly Mr. Winters. Mrs. Winters left me in charge of her gift shop. I make all the decisions around here when she or Ms. Hilda isn't around. So sir, you might want to remember that, sir!" Alex statement ignited a personal vendetta in Sturgis Winters his rage of anger went out against Alex, Sturgis struck back harder using words to hurt Alex, he started off by saying, "Hey Fritz, I heard you have a new bike?" Alex was about to hand Fritz his wrapped boxes of candy so he could leave. Alex didn't want Fritz to answer that or any other question Sturgis had for him. He just wanted him to take his packages, hurry up and leave the shop. He was sick and tired of seeing, hearing about that bike. But Sturgis used the right words to stop Fritz from leaving the shop.

He mentioned the bike. Fritz paused in his steps stating, "Yes, sir as a matter of fact I do," he remarked. "I heard it was real nice!" said Sturgis. "It is and I think so," Fritz replied. "I bet it goes fast! I bet you with your girl have fun riding on it?" taunted Sturgis, "Well sir…It does and we do, as I mentioned earlier to you sir she's not officially my girl, not just yet. But as a matter of fact, we do have fun bike riding. I let her use one of my other bikes when we go riding. And I'm going to invite her to ride with me on Wednesday on the bluffs. That's why I need the candy today. There I'm going to asked her to be my girl," Fritz proudly announced. Alex was crushed! His self-esteem was diminishing! Sturgis could see it in his face and he was adding more verbal hurt to Alex. "Why…your bike sounds like the one I had when I was a young man your age. Would you please describe your new bike in more detail but this time a little louder? I'd appreciate it. My hearing hasn't been too good this morning." Sturgis said, using Fritz's words as his ammunition. "As you wish, sir," Fritz was proud to reply. Sturgis watched Alex slowly becoming frustrated, losing his grip his nerves slightly unraveling. "What color is your bike? Does it go fast? Are the wheels spokes shiny? "I bet they are!" Sturgis interjected. "Does your new bike have a basket to carry items like chocolate candy for your special girl?" Sturgis at this point was doing his best to finish breaking away at Alex's last bit of confidence. Fritz stood speaking, shouted loud in detail about his new bike, bragging about its performance and speed. Sturgis kept instigating, feeding jealous words down the throat of Alex against Fritz in retaliation for Alex's true remarks he made to him moments earlier. His last two questions to Fritz were devastating to Alex. "Oh Fritz... How much did your bike cost and does your potential girl's first name start with the letter "P?" Fritz was hesitant to speak on those questions, but he eventually did replying. "Sir, I can't disclose the dollar amount for the purchase of my new bike. But I can say with honesty the average young man my age could not afford my bike on a mere shop salary. And the answer to your last question is... Yes!" Alex's heart dropped to the floor. His feelings were numb...his body felt limp as he left the room, trying to keep his manly image, pretending to have something in his eye. He did...tears. And in his dreams that night Alex could still hear Fritz ranting loud about his new bike. And all of this was orchestrated by Sturgis Winters.

When Ya'vett arrived at Nan's gift shop Fob the beggar was near. He approached her as Warren went to retrieve his wallet he had left inside their carriage. "Money for a starving man," Fob spoke with humiliation. Then a soft pleasant voice answered him. "I doubt seriously sir if you're starving but here's something. I know it will help," Ya'vett politely said. Warren walking toward Ya'vett said to the beggars, "No money! Move on! Stop mooching! Why don't you get busy with getting an honest job to work for your money like everyone else," Warren voiced, wiping off his coat with a handkerchief because one of the beggars with dirty hands touched his arm. "We've got to do something about these street beggars. We've already addressed the constable about this matter. And they assured us something was going to be done. But, my question is when? When are they going to alleviate this serious problem? Why are they still dragging their feet? They've had enough time and money to rid this unfortunate situation. So, now I see I'll have to use my influence. And, Ya'vett dear without a doubt I'm sure they are responsible for all these burglaries around here. They have to be!" Warren strongly expressed, putting his thick wallet inside his suit pocket, buttoning it. "Now, dear do you know that to be true?" Ya'vett said, adding, "They're just poor, hungry human beings trying to survive in a lifestyle they only know," "Well, that might be. But, it still doesn't change my opinion about them and let me share this with you too, if you hand money to a man like that.

You are handing him a reason not to work. Besides, they all know you give to them, all the time. They know that it's easy to get money from you at any time," Warren augured. Ya'vett was quick to reply. "Yes! You're right! But remember this. It's my money and I'll do with it as I wish!" she expressed, walking inside Nan's Gift Shop. "My words, welcome back! How was your trip abroad?" Hilda asked, Ya'vett told Hilda the trip was scenic, spoiling and relaxing. "I got a chance to meet the rest of Warren's wonderful family. They were all excited to meet me and are looking forward to our lovely wedding in the spring." "I'm glad you came by today because the gift shop is now closed on Wednesday. Hilda stated. "Oh…why is that?" they asked? Hilda went on to say, "Well it seems Mr. Winters being a newlywed and all wants it that way so he can spend more private time with the Mrs." "Oh, my how romantic, see, Warren dear I told you we should come today," Ya'vett said. "Yes, dear, you were right!" he replied.

Sturgis was curious. He overheard his name mentioned along with the names of others he'd met. So he got up from the kitchen table and went into the other room. To secretly look again at the faces of people he'd met in the restaurant some time ago. He wanted to put names to faces. Ya'vett saw him enter the room. "Well…good afternoon Mr. Winters. We pleasantly meet again," Ya'vett said, extending her hand for Sturgis to shake or kiss, forgetting he was blind. And he almost reached for her hand to kiss it then he caught himself. But what he did next he couldn't fake. Sturgis was captivated by her mere presence, overtaken by Ya'vett's natural beauty, dropped his teacup on the gift shop floor. Slightly, trembling, his voice cracking as he spoke, "Please excuse me for my clumsiness," Sturgis said, stuttering and trying to keep it together. "Oh, don't worry about it Mr. Winters," Hilda said, rushing over with a clean white towel. "I'll clean it up, sir." She continued to say. "Oh, oh…yes," he faintly spoke. Then Hilda asked. "Did, you get any tea on your dress Ms. La'Cure?" Hilda and Ya'vett were both looking at her dress for spilled tea stains? "No, Ms. Hilda I don't see any," she answered. *"Miss Ya'vett La' Cure, so that's what she looks like. Enchanting, Artfully, Lovely,"* he whispered. "How do you, do Mr. Winters?" Ya'vett asked." "And how is Mrs. Winters? Warren inquired Sturgis stood speechless looking at Ya'vett lost for words *"How lovely she is. Is she real?"* he was thinking. "How is Mrs. Winters?" again she asked, "Huh, who? Mrs. Who," Sturgis softly replied. "Mrs. Winters your wife my good man!" Warren strongly interjected. "Oooh yeah, her, you mean her. Shee'saaah? She's okay." Sturgis was still mesmerized by the natural beauty and loveliness of Ya'vett La' Cure, he searched for words to answer them, slowly coming to himself saying, "We, oh aahh, we received a post from her last week. She said all is well. Tessa had a healthy boy." "Marvelous," Ya'vett happily said. "And a healthy girl," Oh my goodness! How double wonderful! Twins! Now that's great news, Mr. Winters. And do give Mrs. Winters, Tessa, along with her growing family our best will you please?" Smiling Ya'vett requested. "I shall do just that in my next script to her. I'll have Hilda convey your joyous sentiments," Sturgis expressed as he remained smitten by Ya'vett's pure loveliness. Sturgis had to excuse himself from the room taking a few steps forward. He wanted to look back to make sure she was as lovely as he had seen, but he couldn't because of his pretend blindness. He waited until he got into the next room and seated himself and looked across at her. Gazing, watching Ya'vett's every move, taken by her charm, grace and beauty, falling in love with her.

Hilda had to excuse herself from the room but before leaving she informed Ya'vett and Warren that she would be right back informing Alex, "Hey Alex, I'll be there in a minute don't forget we have to do the paperwork for the bank deposit today, remember we're closed tomorrow," Hilda shouted to him leaving almost to enter the room in which Alex was seated waiting on her. Then Ya'vett called Hilda back into the shop needing a price for a portrait. She gave them a price then told them to take their time in choosing paintings also to let her know if they needed to see more because Mrs. Winters had a nice variety to choose from. Hilda had to go again to help Alex with banking business which included counting all the money for this week's and last week's bank deposit. When she finally returned the couple still hadn't made their portrait selection. So Hilda started to work on placing brightly polished musical jewelry boxes in the shop window for customers to see and buy. Alex told Hilda he needed to leave a little early because he had a few stops to make before the bank closed. She nodded her head yes to Alex. "Well, Warren how do you like this one, dear?" Ya'vett asked. "I don't!" he replied. "Now here's one I like...What do you think about this one Ya'vett?" "Sorry dear it would hang nicely if we were going to be living in a barn." she replied. "What about these?" "Nope" "Hu Au...not in my house you won't," "Are you kidding, me?" Ya'vett and Warren were still undecided when Hilda finished her window display. Ms. Hilda as you can see to confirm "He has a different taste in art than mine," Ya'vett expressed. "And since, we cannot come to an agreement I think the best thing for us to do is come separately. I will be back on Thursday to make my art choices. Then Warren can come back on Friday to make his. Will that be alright with you Ms. Hilda?" Ya'vett asked. "That will be just fine with me," Hilda replied. "Good then!" They both said, looking at each other smiling. "So, I will see you on Thursday, Ms. Hilda," Ya'vett said, putting paintings down on the counter. "And I will see you on Friday," Warren added. "That will be perfect. See you then," Hilda replied smiling as they left the shop. Alex was still gathering his belongings to make the bank deposit run. "I'm leaving now ma'am," he said. "You got everything Alex?" Hilda asked. "Yes ma'am!" He replied. "Okay then, see you on Thursday, bright and early!" "Alright, Mrs. Hilda," he said. Rushing out the door in the direction of the bank but he arrived at the bank not on Tuesday as usual but on Wednesday instead.

Alex stood nervous at the table his hand was shaking as he tried to fill out a new deposit slip. The dollar amount he wrote down on the new deposit slip did not match the dollar amount Hilda counted at the gift shop. He put in less money. Promising to give it all back before Mrs. Winter's returned. Alex was counting on future repayment strategies, coming from prepay days, tips and his small savings. He was sure he could put all the money back in time. As he stood filling out a new deposit slip strangely, he could hear the words of Mr. Toliver…"Alex…" "Huh," he answered. Looking to his right, then to his left…*"Be a man in good standing. Be of good conscience. Be honest. Do that what is right. Show integrity and that integrity will preserve mankind."* "Huh? Mr. Toliver," he said. "Where are you?" Alex stopped writing. He put down the fountain pen. Looking again to his right then to his left and not seeing anyone he waited a few minutes then resumed writing. Again he heard the words of Mr. Toliver…"Be honest. Do what is right." "What?" Alex said, stopping again looking behind him, this time. He saw no one. So he started writing again. "Alex!" …the voice was louder this time. *"Show integrity and that integrity will preserve mankind."* "Yes, sir," Alex said tearing up the new deposit slip and reaching in to his pocket for the old one. But in an instant his mind flashed back to Fritz's new bike. Alex became agitated, jealous and angry all over again. So he picked back up the fountain pen and resumed writing on a new deposit slip tearing up the old one putting it into the trash can His thinking was…If I put back all the money, I'm not really stealing. Alex mind was set he was determined to out-do Fritz at any cost. And Mr. Toliver's words of morality with good conduct flew right over the consciousness of Alex.

Later, coming out of the tailor shop Alex smiled wearing his new clothes while carrying a bundle under his left arm. Walking to Ingram's bikes when the words of Mr. Toliver came to Alex again, but this time even louder than ever! *"Be a man of good conscience, Alex! Show integrity!"* He stopped in the middle of the street… "Huh…where are you?" He said looking around for the man behind the voice. Standing next to him, he could see Mr. Toliver, *"Be a man of good conscience, please!"* Alex dropped his bundle of clothes. He hurried back in the direction of the tailor shop. Only to be distracted by Penny's laughter him seeing her riding on Fritz's new bike. Alex immediately turned back around and headed in the direction of Ingram's bike shop. Entering he said, "I want the newest the most expensive bike you have in your shop. Spare no cost!" Alex almost shouted. Concerned Mr. Ingram asked, "Are you sure that's what you want, Alex?" "Yes sir, I'm definitely sure," he answered. "Well…then I have just the one you're looking for. It came in this morning. But I have to warn you Alex…it's expensive." "At this point Mr. Ingram that doesn't really matter, but what does matter is can this bike out race any bike you've ever sold?" Alex asked. Waiting before answering Alex, Mr. Ingram replied with caution. "Why, Yes…yes, young man." Mr. Ingram replied. Alex lowered his voice for the next question… "Aumm can it. Oh… Aah out race any bike you've ever sold here, lately? "Well? It all depends," Mr. Ingram scratching his beard said. "Well… Alex softly asked. "What about Fritz's new bike can da' it out race that one?" "Ooh, I see. That's it! Mr. Ingram remarked, taking sometime before answering Alex …then said. "Well… Alex why, Why! Yes! Yes! Alex I believe it can!" Alex smiled. then loudly said…"Good then! I'll take it!" "Okay then!" Mr. Ingram replied, grabbing hold to the handlebars of Alex's new bike wheeling it near the counter by the shop's front door. When paying for his bike Alex exposed a large sum of money. "Well… Mr. Alex, aren't we a rich lad today with new fancy clothes. And now a fancy new bike too?" Mr. Ingram remarked. "Well, I suppose so sir, and thank you for the bike," Alex said hurrying out the bike shop. "Oh, hey Alex, before I forget if you don't like the way the bike rides you can exchange it for another one, tomorrow," He shouted, as Alex rode off into the direction of the bluffs.

The sun was still up when Alex arrived at the bluffs. Fritz was waiting for his girl. He could see Alex, coming up he waited until Alex got closer then said, "Alex what are you doing up here?' Fritz asked. "What do you mean what am I doing up here, Fritz? Ah, you don't own the bluffs too," Alex replied. "How do you know?" smiling Fritz remarked. "Hey… Alex that's a nice bike you have there. Who'd you steal it and those new clothes from?" Fritz joking said "Never, you mind all of that Fritz. I'm up here to race for your girl and that's all you need to know!" Alex shouted. "My girl?" Fritz chuckled once, laughed, saying, "Why, my girl, Alex?" "Because she's mine," Alex quickly replied. "Oh, is that so," Fritz remarked. He wanted to know more, asking Alex, "I see and does she know that?" "Well, no not just yet, but!" Alex said, slow in his answer to Fritz. "Ooh! Well then Alex in that case…she's anybody's girl, right?" Fritz stated. Alex had no reply. "Now, tell me this Alex. Are you sure you want to race me?" Fritz was arrogant in his, asking. "Why is that so hard to believe? I'm up here aren't I?" Alex shouted back at Fritz. "Indeed you are," said Fritz pausing a moment to think, "Let me see," he said. "Let me… I know! I got it, Alex!" I'll tell you what? Let's make this race a little more interesting old sport." "Oh? Go on. I'm listening," Alex replied. "Let's see? The winner of this race gets the girl and servitude from the loser for one year, agreed?" Fritz extended his hand for Alex to shake in agreement. Alex thought about it then answered, "Agreed!" They both shook hands saying, "Sealed with a gentlemen's agreement!" "Sealed," they both shouted. Fritz told Alex they would start and finish at the old abandoned windmill. "We must stay on our bikes. If one of us falls to the ground that person is automatically disqualified, losing the race. We must pass Strouss' pumpkin patch all the way to the north end of the bluffs, passing the lighthouse. Three laps will be the qualifying distances. Understood?" Fritz asked. Seeking clarity, "Understood." Alex replied. But what Alex didn't know is that it rained heavy on the bluffs that night before and the thick grass was extremely slippery to an inexperienced rider.

They mounted their bikes then… "Go!" Yelled Fritz! Alex took off first racing at high speeds, skidding a few times on the moist grass, but keeping his balance on the bike, zooming pass the lighthouse. He was a full lap ahead of Fritz, winning the first two laps passing Strouss' pumpkin patch for the third qualifying run. He was headed toward the old abandon windmill for a sure win. When all of a sudden his bike front wheel hit a wet soggy patch of grass speeding out of control sending Alex and his bike over the edge, tumbling over and over, hitting everything in its path, skidding and yelling all the way down until he landed at the button of the bluffs, there he lay wet, dazed, with a sprained finger \with cuts and bruises to his body. His new bike bent beyond repair. Alex drifted into semi-unconsciousness. Fritz waited a few minutes. Then went over to the edge of the bluff he yelled down to Alex three times, "Alex, are you alive? I say there chap are you alive? Alex! Alex! Wake up!" Fritz shouted down to Alex from on top of the bluffs. Alex took some time to regain consciousness. Then he responded on Fritz's third yell by saying "What…What did you say, Hilda? Yesss… I think so," He replied rubbing the back of his aching neck and head. Fritz laughed and shouted to Alex, "Alex, I've been called many of names but never a Hilda. I'm not Hilda. I'm Fritz!" Alex was still dazed not standing up right away. But before speaking again Fritz pondered his words this time a little longer. Taking in a deep breath, he was relieved that Alex was alright and alive. Further commenting, "My good man let this losing lesson make you wiser, stronger and a lot smarter. Take these painful words along with you in your pain of defeat… *Up here championships are won by the wealthy, the rich, and not the poor or uninvited.* Oh, and da' Priscilla along with, myself will be expecting your services on tomorrow, starting at noon. You will start by cleaning our fresh catch of the day!" Fritz shouted. "Priscilla?" Alex still dazed, whispered. "Yes! Priscilla. Priscilla Brightten, the Great Granddaughter of Lady Brightten." Alex paused a moment before speaking. Then spoke slowly in his reply, "Oooh that P…" he sighed. Alex then panicked, whispering, "The money! The money!" he slowly stood to his feet limping from his fall injuries, walking alongside his damaged bike using it as a crutch for the long walk back into town.

As he walked Alex realized what a blind, selfish, dishonest person he had become. He then thought about Penny, having to come to terms with his foolish, costly, mistake he'd made over the wrong girl. But he didn't have time to feel sorry for himself or his injuries, for too long, because he needed to get back into town as fast as he could. He also needed a place to rest his aching body too and it wasn't long before he found one. Alex soon came upon a group of roadside beggars, not knowing that there were thieves and tricksters in the bunch. "Double your money! Double it!" Hey! You lad… Stop here! Get a chance to double your money!" One beggar shouted. Alex stopped he limped over to see if he could win back some, if not all money he had stolen from the gift shop.

Badly needing to replace it and…fast. "Now…how is this game played?" Alex asked going over to a small group near the table top. "First off lad, are you alone? One trickster asked. "Why…Yes, I'm alone!" Alex replied. "Good!" They said. "Why'd you asked me that question?" Alex wanted to know. "Oh Well…because … Ah! Umm! We wouldn't want you ah to have to share your winnings with anyone, else. That's why I asked." "That's right!" one thief said. Who was quick to back up his friend's statement to Alex, "He's, right!" Another trickster stood next to Alex wearing a big grin on his face. He too agreed with what was told to Alex. Alex felt good about his possibilities of winning in this game. So he listened as the trickster explained to him how the game is played. He started off by saying… "Now…this is a special game. It isn't for everyone. Only special people can play this game," the oldest trickster said. While the others agreed in tangent. "So first before we get started. I need to find out one very important fact and that fact is…if you have enough money to play this very special game?" He stated to Alex. "Well," Alex said. How much money do I need?" "Well, how much do you have? I only asked this question to you because you might not have enough money to play this game young lad. You do know this game isn't just for any or everybody. Remember I told you that moment ago, this game is just for special ones," the oldest trickster said. "Yes, you did tell me that I forgot," Alex replied. "Yes…you have to be very special to play this game," The others said. In Alex's desperateness and their skillfulness in lying he gave in to their deceptive word maneuvering which forced him to foolishly pull out his thick roll of money. "Wow!" One thief shouted unable to contain himself almost losing his glasses in the excitement after seeing Alex's large wad of money. However, the thief was able to catch his glasses before they fell off his face onto the ground. He also stood grinning looking at Alex's money. They were all excited at the sight of Alex's large roll of funds. "Well, then I think he has enough. Wouldn't you fella agree?" *"Wow! I' agree," Me, too,"* "I do too," what about the rest of you guys? The leader asked. *"We do too,"* Each of them having different comments but all were agreeing on one thing. They patting Alex on the back confirming he had enough money to play this game "Yep! It looks as if you do have enough money to play this special game. You're in luck, lad. You couldn't be luckier," the leader said. Smiling, rubbing his hands together as he begins to explain the game to Alex. "Now, pay close attention young lad. This game is quite easy!" the leader said. He went on to tell Alex how to play the game while another trickster observing was ever so eager to agree, then that same trickster stop looking and started juggling eight big shiny red apples in the air laughing. But it was that short thin member in the bunch, which held in his hand a musical tambourine hitting it on the palm of his hand. Then holding it high into the air shaking it dancing, laughing, as the small sparkling diamond-cut brass cymbals on the side of it kissed with a sweet sound of victory. "You see this little pea? I'll place it under here then move it around? Now…all you have to do is guess which walnut shells the pea under; one, two, or three! That's it!" He told Alex. "That's it's? That's all I have to do?" Alex quickly replied. He, Alex was surprised to learn just how easy the game really was. "That's it and that's all!" The trickster said. "Aaah, that ain't nothing. That's easy," replied Alex. "See, I told you it was easy. That's all you have to do," a thief replied looking at Alex with a happy face then to his fellas with a sincere look, a wink and a smile. The game got started and if felt as if it went on for what seemed like hours. With the youngest trickster doing a special celebrated dance for Alex, he too would hit his tambourine and dance around the table every time Alex won. While he smiled, watching the long strands of red, yellow, and green, ribbons, attached to it swirl high into the air. They too danced to his music. As the others clapped and patted Alex on the back, cheering him on, encouraging him to keep playing, inflating his ego. And he did. But when it was over, they had tricked Alex out of every dollar he had. Alex was broke. He had no money left and was still hurting from his injuries. Now he was hurting even greater from, stupidity. He watched with sadness as the tricksters, beggars, thieves laughed, dividing up amongst themselves. Their winnings from him…the money he stole from the gift shop. They ignored Alex as they collected their wooden barrel table top, empty walnut shells along with a half bag of peas. They headed up the road. To a new spot waiting for the next fool to come along leaving Alex behind to sulk in his vain stupidity which almost brought him to tears. As he sat on the ground going through his pockets trying to find some money somewhere inside of them, but there was none to be found except a worthless wad of cotton lint.

Observing, all of this was the odd man that lived under a bush. Alex tried passing him without being seen. "Stop! What's your rush?" he said. "I saw what happened. I see you're hurt in more ways than one. Here I have just what you need this small jar of magical ointment for your cuts and it's almost free, but sorry nothing for your bruised ego." The odd man said. "No! No! No!" frustrated Alex shouted. "Nothing is free! It will cost me something and I have no more money left! But…thank you, kind sir," Alex said about to leave to head back into town. But he was curious. So Alex stopped then said. "Sir, may I ask you a question, please?" "Me?" the odd man replied. "Yes, sir you," Alex said. The odd man took in a deep breath letting it out acting in such a way. As if he already knew what Alex was about to asked him, "Ask… On." The odd man said. Alex was slow to speak yet he said. "Well…ah why do they call you the odd man and why do you live under this bush?" Alex inquired. "Why?" The odd man whispered, and not responding to Alex's question right away letting minutes pass by. Then the odd man said, "Are you sure you want to know the answer to that question?" "Why…why yes sir. I think so," Alex replied, he was somewhat hesitant. "No! Are you sure?" The odd man soft but firmly asked. It only took Alex a few seconds to respond. "Yes! …Why, Yes! Sir, I do!" "There's no reversing your request," the odd man strangely said. "Yes! I'm sure,"

Alex shook his head yes. "Okay…then if you must," in an instant the odd man emerged from under the bush with a raven resting on his left shoulder. The odd man appeared wearing soiled burlap covering for clothing, hiding what appeared to be feathers on his body, which seemed to be forcing their way through the dry rotted woven burlap fabric seams. He was missing ears, thumbs and his faced displayed a big, thick, bright, orange hard curved bird beak for a mouth, standing on rough stony talons for feet. The odd man turned himself he stood facing Alex in silence. Alex couldn't move. He was frozen from fright as if his heart stopped and dropped to the ground. Terrified, unable to speak, only a cold silence stood between them. "Now… You see…why?" the raven said, answering Alex in a deep human voice. "Ubba, Ubba, eee…Yesss…I see," said Alex with widened-eyes, panting for breath, his body shaking from fear. Alex took a hard swallow he tried to find saliva somewhere in his mouth to scream but couldn't. Instead he immediately jumped on his broken bike to rush off forgetting it was damaged throwing it to the ground leaving it there. Hurrying his limping walk faster than before, Alex did not stop until he got some ways down the road. The odd man rushed to the middle of the road shouting, waving his balled thumb-less fist yelling, "Wait! Come back here you little thief! If you can't accept the answer, then don't ask the question. And you better pay back that money you stole," hysterically laughing he said.

Tired and scared Alex stopped to rest again. Later when it was safe he went back to retrieve his bike. Further down the road he changed before reaching town, putting back on his old dry clothes. He hid along the roadside under a pile of dry leaves before going up to the bluffs to meet Fritz. He wiped his face with the new, wet torn clothing and smoothed out the wrinkles on his old clothing to look presentable. Then he brushed down his hair with his hands. He entered Ingram's bike shop. "I'm sorry! I'm in business to make money not lose it. You know I only sell new bikes … Not used or broken ones," Mr. Ingram told Alex. Alex begged he pleaded for Mr. Ingram to take back the bike for any price. Ingram thought about it then said a firm, "No!" Alex was disappointed leaving the bike shop. He then took his damaged bike and hid it inside an abandoned farm shed not far from Ingram's hiding it behind stacked, bales of rotting hay from the rains, hoping no one would find it until he could decide on what to do with it. And Mr. Wetzel, holding a pair of long, sharp metal scissors, chased Alex out of his tailor shop, yelling, "You must be mad coming back here demanding your money back for those ol' wet, torn, muddy, stained, clothes! Now you get out of here! Stay away! And don't you come back her again!" Mr. Wetzel shouted as he threw Alex's newly damaged clothes into the street. Alex was exhausted, tired with no place to go. So he went back to the old farm shed making a bed out of some dry hay and took a short nap. Just before midnight he was at the gift shop door drenched from pouring rain, pounding, banging and knocking on the door, yelling, "Mr. Winters…let me in I need your help! I've done something dishonest, something

terribly wrong! Please help me Mr. Winters! Open the door, please!"
Sturgis stayed silent, standing quiet on the other side of the solid oak gift
shop door peering down at Alex through a crack in the closed door
window shutters. He heard young Alex's pleas for help but ignored them.
Sturgis just smiled, turned and walked away.

When Alex didn't show up to work on time the next work day, Hilda
wasn't alarmed because he had been late before. But when Penny came
looking for Alex saying he did not come home to the orphanage last
night Hilda knew something was terribly wrong. "Hilda! I have great
news! My sight has returned!" Smiling Sturgis said. "You don't say?
How wonderful for you Mr. Winters," Hilda replied, somewhat happy,
somewhat unconcerned. She and her niece Abby always suspected he
could see but had no real evidence of that. But Hilda pretended she was
happy for him anyway. "I'm so glad for you sir. Penny did you hear? Mr.
Winter's sight has returned." "Yes, ma'am I heard that's wonderful Mr.
Winters, I'm glad for you, too sir," Penny politely said. She was happy
for Mr. Winters but seemed to be more concerned about Alex's
wellbeing. She stated again "Yes, I'm very happy for you Mr. Winters
and so will Mrs. Winters when she returns. I'm sure of it!" Hilda wanted
to know if she should send a post informing Mrs. Winters the good news
regarding his sight. "I know she'll want to rush home to share in on your
good news as soon as possible, sir" Hilda asked. "No! No! No! Hilda,
that won't be necessary," Sturgis was quick to reply. "I want to wait, let
this be a big surprise for her when she returns. But in the meantime, look!
Look, ladies. I won't be, needing these dark glasses anymore. Yes, yes,
yes, this is going to be a brand new start for me," Sturgis smiled, feeling
chipper as he dropped, his dark glasses into the trash in front of Hilda
and Penny using them, without them being aware, as witnesses to his
returned sight. "Yes, this is going to be a fantastic day I can hardly wait
to get this day started!" He happily said, grinning, stretching out his
arms and taking in a deep breath. Hilda told Mr. Winters, she was still
concerned about Alex's whereabouts. "That's strange. No one seems to
know where he is," Hilda stated. "Now, Hilda, don't' start worry he'll
show up! Running in here late, making up excuses like he always does!"
Sturgis replied. "Oh, I don't know Mr. Winters. I don't feel good about
this. That doesn't sound like the Alex we know not showing up for
dinner at the orphanage and all. He has always been dependable here
and over there, too. Where can that boy be?" Hilda said. Sturgis quickly
changed the mood in the gift shop by saying, "Now come on Hilda, this
beautiful sunny day just got started. And I got my sight back too. Now
isn't that in itself reason enough to celebrate? So cheer up! Let's not
bring back the rain, okay? Let's not spoil this grand day!" He'll show
up!! Look! Hilda I can see you!" Sturgis smiling said. He was doing his
best to change the subject about Alex by charming Hilda with his words
of compliments. "That's wonderful for real Mr. Winters about your sight
coming back. I'm real glad for you. Now how good is your sight?" Hilda
inquired. "Well, hum? Let me see," he said. "...I can see your lovely

new white blouse. You're pretty pink ruffled apron, your rosy red cheeks. And oh, let's not forget your plump round attractive figure." "Oh! Mr. Winters, please," Hilda blushing said. "Now don't worry, Hilda. Alex will be just fine! Give him time to get here, that's all," Then Sturgis told Penny not to worry either. That when Alex came, he would send him straight over to the orphanage to let everybody know that he was alright. Sadly enough since that statement was spoken by Mr. Winters. Many seasons have come and went. And it seemed no one has seen young Alex. He just vanished.

At, the counter dressed in a new, dark gray suit, wearing fine men accessories, minus the hat, Sturgis Winters waited for Ya'vett's carriage to come. He eagerly watched for her to walk through the gift shop door. But instead Nan's carriage pulled up. "Oh look!" Hilda said in excitement! "It's Mrs. Winters! She didn't tell us she was coming today! Did you know, sir? Did she tell you? She was coming in today?" Hilda happily asked. "Well, I'd… I'd," he replied standing at the counter, firmly clasping his hands together in disappointment, placing them down hard on the glass counter, biting slightly down on his lower lip in disgust. "Yes that's her carriage, sir. Aren't you going to greet Mrs. Winters, sir? Aren't you going to help her with the bags? Then you can tell her yourself about your sight returning. I know she'd be glad to hear it especially coming from you," Hilda happily stated. He was hesitant in no hurry. First taking his time then a quiet deep breath in, he said, "Oh! Her bags, Why…Yes! But, da' I'll let her come up the walk first then I'll go outside to meet her. I want my returned sight to be a big surprise for her." Nan was happy to see her husband after months away. She was kissing him in the face, standing on her tip toes inside the shop door arch trying to reach her husband mouth for a kiss. While still holding onto some of her bags and he, was trying to avoid her kisses, turning his head away saying, "I'm happy to see you too, dear. But I have great news for you. My sight came back last night." "What did you say Sturgis, It did?" Nan was happy for Sturgis which gave her all the more reason to kiss him," But he was hoping that news would stop her from trying to kiss him. And it did. "Oh! Good dear, how wonderful!" smiling she replied, "Sturgis, dear that was going to be my next question to you. I noticed when you came out side you weren't wearing your dark glasses anymore. I missed you immensely dear! And I told you that your sight would return, now didn't I, dear? Oh, Sturgis I'm so excited and glad for you," she expressed. "Well, Yes, you did dear," he said trying to be modest. Then Nan started back trying to kiss him on the lips, again. But Sturgis was determined to finish his say. "Well, to be perfectly honest with you dear. My sight came back a few days ago but I needed to make sure before alarming anyone with false hopes," Sturgis confessed. "Why Mr. Winters! You fooled us for the last two days," Hilda said thinking otherwise that she and her niece, Abby could quite have possibly been correct regarding his ability to see all the time. "I know Hilda. I'm guilty. I should have told you but I needed to make sure. Now it's safe to say my sight is back," grinning he stated. "Well I don't care when it came back. I'm just glad it did my dearest. Now, pay the driver please, Sturgis," Then Nan wittingly commented, "Sturgis dear, you must have known I was coming today." "Why, you'd say that, dear?" he asked. "Because you're dressed so handsomely," she replied. "Oh, you think so? Why thank you dear." He said with innocence. "Oh, by the way Nan dear you didn't mention in your post you were coming today," he said. "I know I didn't. I thought it would be nice to surprise all of you with a sudden return. I have gifts for everyone including Abby and Hilda I know you will make sure that Abby gets her gift." "Yes, ma'am I sure will," Hilda said, with a smile

Hilda was so happy to see Mrs. Winters she gave her a big hug with tears in her eyes. "Glad you're home ma'am. Good you're back," Hilda said. Yes, and I'm glad to be back Hilda," Nan replied taking off her gloves and shawl putting them on the sofa. "By the way where is Alex?" Nan asked. Sturgis was quick to say, "Oh, we're waiting for him to get here dear you know that Alex. He has a record for lateness," Sturgis commented. "Well… yes, dear you're right about that," smiling Nan said, sitting down, tired from her long trip. Then they all wanted to know how Tessa's new babies were. "I'm so exhausted from my trip. First, let me hand out these gifts. Here's yours Hilda and that one is for Abby. I'll put Alex's on the counter so when he comes in he can see it. Sturgis I'll give you yours tonight after dinner, dear," Nan said, smiling. "Now to answer your questions about the twins they are just fine. Their names are Clarissa and her brother's name is Trent junior. They are beautiful babies. Now, if you don't mind I'm going to take a long hot bath and lie down to rest. When, I awake I will be happy to tell all of you about my trip sharing more about the twins. Along with any other questions each of you may have. Now, I'll see all of you in a little while." Nan shared with them. Sturgis waited until he and Nan were alone, to whisper, "Now, seriously dear how was your trip really?" He wanted to know expressing in a somewhat romantic tone. Nan stopped to looked, at him. She whispered back. "Lonely, very lonely for you Sturgis and if you like you may draw my bath, right now," He smiled then panicked. He thought about Ya'vett's carriage was to arrive soon. "Right Now?" he frantically answered. "Yes, dear right now," Nan was sensuous in her answer. Sturgis was confused, he stood thinking. Should I or shouldn't I? He was anxious for two reasons one Miss La' Cure, the other Mrs. Winters, his wife. He was expecting Ms. La' Cure to be the next person to walk through that gift shop door. And he wanted to be up front at the counter to meet her as she walked in. When all of a sudden…"I got you, you're not getting away, this time!" Hilda said. "Got who?" Nan shouted. A little fella who was being held by Hilda and he was trying to resist her hold. He had on clothes but the shoes were too big for him. He was using braded strips of fabric in the place of a belt to keep his pants up. "He must have sneaked in behind Penny this morning then hid out in the shop somewhere. He's the one that's been taking our snow globes. I just caught him trying to take another one out of the shop. See, here it is!" Hilda said holding the snow globe in her right hand while grabbing on to the little thief's collar with her left hand. "He's swiped three of them already!" Hilda stated. "Oh my," Nan expressed. She further asked the boy "Is this true. What Ms Hilda just said did you. Did you take them?" He was afraid to answer at first. Then he finally said, "Yes, ma'am. It's true." "Well in that case everyone. Let me freshen up a bit, lie down for a few moments to rest my tired eyes. Then I'll come back to address this matter. Hilda, take him into the kitchen. He looks as though he's hungry as if he hasn't eaten in a while. So, please fix him something nice and hot to eat. Mr. Winters can cover the counter. Oh, Sturgis, should you need any help, please let us know," "Yes, dear I will, Oh and da" Nan dearest before I forget glad you're home. Do you still want me to prepare your bath?" Sturgis asked. "No, Not, now. Perhaps later," smiling Nan said, further saying, "I'm afraid I wouldn't enjoy it right now anyway," Nan was frustrated but she tried to keep a smile on her face leaving the room heading down the hall to the bedroom.

In the meantime, Ya'vett walked into the gift shop unnoticed everyone else was in other rooms of the shop. So she went over to the paintings, carefully looking at each one putting aside the ones she was going to buy. "Oh! Ms. La' Cure," Sturgis said. He was startled, with happiness and disappointment. He wanted to be at the counter to greet her, when she came into the shop as he had planned, "I'm so sorry Miss La' Cure I didn't hear you come in," He softly replied looking at her, whispering *a portrait of loveliness, a rare sculpture of beauty*. Please accept my apologies. I didn't hear the shop bell sound. I was in the other room unpacking these candlestick holders. Forgive me, please" he said starring at Ya'vett, enjoying her pure innocence, her natural beauty. "Well, my goodness Mr. Winters I see you're not wearing your dark glasses anymore. Now, don't tell me your eyesight has returned!" Ya'vett said in disbelief, smiling at Sturgis, clapping her hands together in jubilation, hugging him in the excitement and, he embracing her longer than necessary. "Why, yes it did!" He happily replied, "How wonderful! Oh, I'm so happy for you, Mr. Winters! And does Mrs. Winters know?" she asked. "Ah…yes she does! As a matter of fact her carriage arrived just this morning." He said, "Well…good for you, both and how does she feel about your sight returning? Is she excited, too?" Ya'vett asked. Sturgis was hesitant to answer at first then he replied, "Oh! Yes she was extremely excited too," "Good!" Ya'vett replied, smiling then said, with excitement and enthusiasm, "Now, tell me Mr. Winters, tell me the truth. Can you clearly see me or are you faking?" Sturgis was surprised by her request he almost dropped the brass candlestick holder on to the glass counter he was holding in his hands but he gently placed it down thinking, knowing he had to stop the world to carefully answer this one crucial, important question for Ms. La' Cure. Realizing he had to send a strong message of interest making his intentions clearly known to her so he gently eased close to her. She was surprised but not frightened as he spoke softly, directly in her face, looking into her eyes. He softly said, "Yes, I can clearly see you and I see beauty, loveliness in a shapely form. I can hold it in my arms, caress it. Touch it with tender passion. Taste its pleasure, admire it up close or from afar and my tireless appetite for it would be endless. And I would willingly be its relentless servant pleasing it in any way she so desires," After Ya'vett heard those words from Sturgis Winters, she was almost spellbound. As he used strong alluring romantic innuendoes pressing himself against her body whispering deep, enticing tones of promises in her ear. Ms. La Cure wanted to leave at that point but couldn't. Her passion was stirred it had united with his. She loved the entrapping words that flowed from the lips of Sturgis Winters. So she stayed, softly panting, wanting to hear more. But hearing Hilda moving around in the kitchen they both became a little frightened thinking Hilda could enter at any moment. And seeing them in such close contact might demand an explanation. So, Sturgis quickly changed the mood with his conversation and she followed along, "Although my sight has recently returned I can clearly determine a good artist's work when I see it. And it seems to me that Zines is a much better artist than Ni. But this is only my personal opinion. What do you think Ms. La'Cure?" He said looking at her with a smile on his face. Then he kissed her on the cheek and she smiled back. Later he asked Ya'vett if she wanted paintings in watercolor or oil, helping to further change the mood. She answered by saying, "Why, Mr. Winters at this moment I don't really know what to think." Ya'vett answered she was showing slight signs of nervous perspiration coming through her long-sleeve silk, light-cream colored blouse. In need of help she reached inside the left wrist sleeve on her blouse grabbing for the white lace handkerchief to fan her face. In trying to deal with controlling her emotions that was spinning out of control. Sturgis knew it. He could see it. He welcomed it. As he tried to dogmatically chip away at what was left of her wall of virtue. Ya'vett attempted to walk off again from Sturgis. But he softly, firmly grabbed her hand pulling her back close to him, kissing her, pressing against her body with his, trying to make her commit to meeting him for a secret romantic rendezvous. Although, Ya'vett found Sturgis' flirtations flattering, welcoming. She wouldn't commit to meeting him. Sturgis was frustrated, because of his last two failed attempts with Ya'vett. So he decided to change the mood back to business. Trying to catch her off guard, the two of them stood close at the counter still pretending to be interested in paintings. "Let me see that portrait Ms. La' Cure… I hope the artist signed his work this time. Please, hand me that last painting?" he asked. Ya'vett, did she handed Sturgis the painting and without her knowing his next move. Sturgis quickly took hold to her hands, then her waist, pressing against her body, kissing her, with great passion but this time on the back of her neck, using his tongue, his kisses as soft, gentle soothing fingers while whispering in Ya'vett's ear. She was totally caught off guard. And taken in by Sturgis' strong sexual advances Ya'vett was ready to say "yes" to his request for a secret romantic meeting. When…"Don't forget I'm outside waiting, dear." Warren said, tired of waiting in the carriage. He decided to go into the shop to see why the long wait. They broke apart from each other just in time. "Yes, he did. He did," Ya'vett spoke with nervousness in her speech and her behavior. Almost repeating herself when she answered Sturgis. "Yes, he did. Yes, yes, see he did. Mr. Winters. Aah, he did sign his work, aah see." she replied, searching for words, surprised by her fiancé abrupted entrance into the gift shop which left her almost speechless. Ya'vett was glad yet disappointed Warren entered the shop when he did. She moved her hand away from Sturgis' cleared her throat then moved down to the other end of the counter. As if to be looking at more paintings. Warren stood in the shop, silent. His eyes were listening they were gleaming, looking at Ya'vett's behavior while watching Sturgis with great suspicion.

He could tell something was strange. She was nervous, different. Her clothes were slightly wrinkled her lipstick smeared, but he didn't draw any conclusions, not yet. With him inside Ya'vett was careful she kept a safe distance between her and Sturgis. Warren was perturbed he got right in the face of Sturgis, speaking to him in a sincere but joking manner, "Well, Mr. Winters, I see you have your sight back. How convenient for you. Interesting, I must say." Sturgis had no comment. "Are you finished selecting your artwork, dear?" Warren asked. "Well, almost Warren. I've chosen four pieces but as you know we need a total of ten. These will have to do for now." She said trying not to appear or sound nervous. While commenting in a joking manner, "I'm glad you came in when you did dear. My eyelids were starting to become tired and heavy," putting her hands up to her eyes, rubbing them. "The colors on the paintings were starting to run together, like a colorful kaleidoscope. It had gotten to the point I didn't know what I was looking at anymore," she said, laughing between words. "I see," Warren was cunning in his reply. "And Warren, dear I think it will be best for me to come back again one day next week to complete my order," Ya'vett said. "Indeed. Hmm.. Let me see. I'll tell you what dear. Why don't, we both come back one day next week together. What do you think about that idea, dear?" Warren stated. Then he looked directly at Sturgis. "I think," she attempted to answer but Sturgis intervened by saying. "I think it would be an honest solution," He responded smiling at Warren. "Until next week Winters," Warren sternly said in his reply to Sturgis. "Thank you Mr. Winters, please give Mrs. Winters our best would you please?" Ya'vett, avoided looking at Sturgis, asked. "You'll be seeing me again Winters you can be sure of it," Warren said helping Ya'vett out of the shop and into their carriage. Sturgis had no reply. He stood inside the opened gift shop door waiting for their carriage to drive off. Then Sturgis pulled Ya'vett's handkerchief out of his vest pocket she dropped on the floor when Warren suddenly entered the shop. He held her handkerchief in his hands looking at it, smiling, gently rubbing it next to his face, kissing it, smelling it and remembering the sweet lingering fragrance of Ms. Ya'vett La. Cure. Sturgis kissed it again, putting her handkerchief back into a pocket. But this time the pocket close to his heart, pressing it once, against his chest. He stood looking in the direction of her moving carriage smiling with pleasure far beyond words, as he slowly closed the gift shop door.

"I only took three of them. I broke one." Little Deek said in the kitchen finishing up his lunch. "What is your name?" Nan asked the boy. She was just awaking from a short nap after her trip. "My name is Little Deek." he said. "Is that your real name?" Hilda asked. "Well, I think so. I don't really know but it could be. Besides that's the only name I've ever answered to." "Where do you live?" Nan asked. "I don't I live on the streets. That's my home," He replied. Hilda asked the boy who's your father? "I don't know that either" They asked about his mother. He told them the snow globes were his mother. "What do you mean by saying that?" Hilda asked looking concerned. They remind him of his mother, the lady inside of them sitting in the carriage with her little boy. He was real hungry that day his mother went to the docks asking people for money for some food. Leaving him and the snow globes in care of a woman that stayed next door. But before his mother left she told Little Deek to keep the snow globe that it was just as valuable as he was and that she'd be right back for them both. "It's been four years now," he said. Nan hugged Little Deek. She told him she was sorry to hear that sad story. And she also wanted to know if he still had any of the snow globes. He told them he did and they were hidden in a secret place. "If, I let you go get them will you return?" Nan asked. "Yes, ma'am!" he replied. "Okay then you can go get them," Nan said. "But wait!" Little Deek said. Almost shouting "Aren't you going to ask me why I'd be coming back with them?" smiling he asked. "Well, if you like," Hilda replied. Then she and Nan looked at each other, each waiting on the other to respond to Little Deek's request. With Nan finally did, asking. "Well, why, Little Deek, why would you be returning with them?" He quickly answered "Because you fed me a good hot meal ma'am and it's been a long time since I had one." He replied. Nan and Hilda laughed at his answer. Even he had to smile, again as he wiped his mouth with the napkin before leaving the table to go retrieve the snow globes.

While Little Deek was gone, Hilda mounted a pair of empty dueling pistols on the shop wall that washed ashore inside wooden crates last year. Little Deek entered carrying the snow globes inside a sack. With curiosity, he asked, "Ms. Hilda do you use those on people that don't pay their bill?" "Oh, No," Sturgis said coming down from one of the aisles inside the shop, "We use them on people who take our snow globes and don't pay for them." "Mr. Winters please…No! Don't say that! You'll frighten the poor child," she said. "Alright Hilda," I was only kidding with the little guy. Hey, Little Deek…forget what I just said, it's not true," laughing Sturgis said. "Mr. Winters," Hilda said. "Okay Hilda, I'm sorry I was just making fun. Isn't that right Little Deek?" he asked. But Little Deek didn't answer back rather he watched Sturgis with caution. As he handed over to him a sack containing snow globes. Little Deek felt real good inside because he kept his promise, his word by coming back with the snow globes Nan was glad, too. However, she told him he would have to work around the shop to make up for the one he broke. "Does lunch come with it, ma'am?" he asked. "Yes, meals come with it," Hilda replied. "Great!" smiling he said. "You can start right now by sweeping the walkway. After that you can pick up outback near the stables. Then help Mr. Winter's around here inside and again outside the shop by cutting some of the small hedges. Especially in front of the gift shop window," Nan said. Sturgis just finished moving a full box of loose shark and whale tooth to the back of the shop because they weren't selling fast enough. Little Deek later dusted shelves containing old sea scrolls, maps, compasses and telescopes. He took the brass collapsible telescope and stretched it out, held it up to his eye looking around the shop having fun with it when his searching led him to the feet, knees then the face of Sturgis. Little Deek hurried he quickly collapse it placing the telescope back onto the shelf.   "I'll take it from here Nan," Sturgis said, after seeing Little Deek in his follies…"I'll show Little Deek what to do around here," Sturgis further, added, reaching for the broom Nan was holding in her hand. Have you ever used a broom one like this before, correctly boy? " Sturgis asked Little Deek in a deep masculine tone to get his attention as they both stood near the front shop door. "I think so sir," Little Deek replied. "You know it's an art to using a broom?" Sturgis said. "No, sir, I didn't know that," Little Deek replied, "Yep and yes it is. But don't worry I'll show you how it's done," Sturgis stated as Little Deek followed him out the gift shop heading near the stables. Nan was still worried. It was getting late. Alex still had not shown up for work. "Hilda, if Alex isn't here in a few more minutes I'll have to go over to the orphanage and speak with Mrs. Hudgemen concerning his whereabouts. I don't know what else to do," she told Hilda. "Yes, ma'am, Mrs. Winters that will be the right thing to do," Hilda answered, looking more concerned than ever about Alex's welfare.

Nan wasn't away from the shop for very long when Mr. Utley sent a messenger over from the bank. "It seems the bank needed a signature on the shop's deposit slip that young Mr. Alex forgot to sign, when he made the deposit a few days ago." Hilda saw the messenger entered the gift shop door. with a document in his hand. "Wait let me get my reading glasses. I'll sign it." smiling, Hilda told him, "That young Mr. Alex, always in a hurry for nothing but late for everything." Hilda hadn't finished speaking those words. When she looked down at the deposit slip, she gasped grabbing her chest having to suddenly sit down. She was devastated. "Ma'am… Are you alright?" The concerned messenger asked. Hilda was hesitant in answering, taking some time to collect her composure, she eventually did, saying. "Yes, yes, I'm okay" Hilda replied. She and her voice were weak devastated from seeing the wrong amount of money deposited in the bank by Alex. He didn't deposit the full amount. Hilda made it a point to always write down every dollar amounts on separate sheets of paper placing them inside the back of the cash drawers in the event she's ever asked to verify deposits it is her private way of record keeping. She specifically remembered the count for that day because it was her youngest nephew's birthday. Hilda entire being was shaken. She felt betrayed at what she discovered, knowing, now that Alex was probably in hiding or he'd left town. Again the messenger said "Ma'am?" Hilda couldn't speak this time. She hurried to sign the slip and gave it back, "Thank you, ma'am and Ma'am are you sure you're alright can I get you anything, before I leave," The bank messenger asked. Hilda shook her head no then smiled. She waited until the messenger was outside, away from the shop. Hilda sat back down again and dropped her face into her folded arms on the desk. And cried, sobbing "Alex! Alex! You didn't have to do this. What's wrong with you child?" She had to painfully realize that Alex was a thief. He'd stolen the gift shop monies and wasn't coming back. With Nan still at the orphanage Hilda knew she would be returning at any minute so not knowing what to do about Alex or the money. Hilda knew she had to tell Nan. But how was she going to tell her? So Hilda decided to practice on how to tell Nan about Alex without causing her too much hurt or disappointment. Hilda looked around the shop for a comfortable stool to sit down on. She sat holding a hand mirror looking into it, talking into it, rehearsing and practicing.

While outside the shop, "Hey Winters, you handle that boom like you sleep with it. You do know that kind of work is for hired help or henpecked husbands. Now, which one are you? Aaa! Why don't you stop wasting your time doing women's work and start making some real big money like a real man," Fob heckled, Sturgis trying to get his attention. "Hey, Winters I've heard of some men that can make you a very rich man, interested?" Sturgis kept silent, ignoring Fob. "Oh, well… When you're ready, you'll know where to find me. I'm always around. Oh, look Winters, you missed a spot. Ha! And don't forget to do the ironing too, lady of the house!" Fob said laughing as he walked off. "Hey! Little Deek!" Fob shouted. "Hey Fob!" Little Deek shouted back. Sturgis asked but waited until Fob was out of ear-shot "Little Deek, do you know him?" "Au Hu," Little Deek replied. "Hmmm," Sturgis sighed but he was curious about Fob's remarks, still looking in the beggar's direction as he put the horses back into the stables. When Nan returned from the orphanage she informed, "Hilda, I got a chance to speak with Mrs. Hudgemen about Alex. We discussed other concerns of mine, as well. She told me Penny was right. Alex did not come in last night, nor has she seen him this morning. Mrs. Hudgemen didn't know where he was but she was sure he was alright. Assuring me when he comes he will get word to me so we can all stop worrying," Nan felt much better but she was still upset about Alex. "Where can that boy, be?" she whispered. Hilda told Nan those were good words to hear. Now she can rest her nerves a little. Nan was so concerned about Alex when she entered the shop she didn't notice right away that Hilda had been crying. "Hilda! I'm so sorry! You've been crying. It isn't Alex is it?" Hilda knew she had to carefully choose her words. So she sat down looking up at Nan saying. "Haven't, seen young Alex yet," Hilda knew she had to come up with a quick reason for her tears. Along with an excuse to leave the gift shop early. Without having to tell Nan about the gift shop money Alex stole. Hilda was aware that kind of news would only break Nan's heart. "Ah…my gout's flaring up again," Hilda said. "That darn pain! Ouch! There its goes again, Ouch," She shouted grabbing her left shoulder pretending to be in pain. Hilda made her mind up that she didn't want to stay at the gift shop or be around Nan knowing if she did she would have to inform her about the bank messenger coming to the shop with everything else surrounding his visit. So later she asked Nan, "Mrs. Winters, ma'am do you mind if I leave for home early today?" Hilda needed to leave the shop, to further give this unfortunate matter a great deal of thought, "Ms. Hilda's not feeling well, at all?" she said. Hilda couldn't betray two close and dearest friends. She also knew staying meant eventually having to tell Nan all about Alex, knowing that painful information would only hurt, and destroyed them both.

"Why, of course not Hilda. Take all the time you need listen don't worry. I'll keep you informed about Alex too," Nan replied. "Yes ma'am," Hilda softly said. "But I'm sure when you come back to work Alex will be back too!" Nan remarked. But Hilda didn't respond to that comment. Rather she changed her mind and decided to tell Nan about Alex anyway. Hilda felt it was the right thing to do. "Ma'am," she said reaching for her sweater then her hat. "Yes?" Nan stopped looking out of the gift shop window for Alex. She turned to face Hilda. Hilda… opened her mouth to tell Nan about Alex's thievery but changed her mind replying, "Oh that's. Oh, well ma'am that's alright Mrs. Winters it's nothing," Hilda stated. "Are you sure?" Nan asked. "Umm hum," Hilda responded. "Oh look! Hilda, there's a stopped carriage out front. You might want to get it before it's gone!" Nan said. "Yes, ma'am, you're right ma'am… I better grab it before someone else does," she answered. "And… I hope you get better Hilda. You look so sad. Are you sure you're okay?" asked Nan. "No Ma'am! I'm not. As a matter of fact I'm not feeling well at all. Hilda taking a few seconds before she spoke…"Now you look here… Mrs. Winters!" Hilda abruptly said, startling Nan. "…Yes! Hilda what is it?" Hilda started again to tell Nan about Alex but she couldn't. "Oh, never mind," she said. Taking in a deep breath, "I just aah need to take something for the pain, that's all," she said, rubbing her left shoulder, again. "Oh, my Hilda, well you better hurry home to do just that!" Nan said walking out with Hilda to her carriage. "Hope you feel better, soon." "Why, thank you, Mrs. Winters I'm sure I will and Good-bye," Hilda said. Looking sad as she boarded her ride for home.

"Hello, Mrs. Winters," Mr. Toliver said approaching Nan seeing her outside the shop saying goodbye to Hilda. "Sorry, Mrs. Winters I'm running a little late today," he said coughing between words. "We're swamped delivering these invitations." He mentioned. "Oh, yes the invitations to the ball, that's right! I almost forgot. Well come right in and rest. Will you have time for a cup of hot tea?" Nan asked. "Well, thank you…maybe half of a cup," he replied. "Mrs. Winters please excuse my coughing," Mr. Toliver said coughing between sipping his cup of tea. The talk and excitement in town is this year's upcoming Governor's Ball in three weeks. "Oh, by the way…did I get one. An invitation I mean?" excited Nan asked. "No! Sorry, Mrs. Winters, nothing for you today. No invitations, as of yet. Mr. Toliver replied. He was in a hurry. "Are you sure?" Nan asked. "Yes, ma'am I'm sure but wait. Mrs. Winters let me double check my bag again to make extra sure. Oh, look! I didn't see this piece of mail," Nan's hopes elevated thinking it might be her invitation that he forgot to deliver. "Oh no…it's just one little post card for you ma'am. Here you go Mrs. Winters," he handing Nan the card. "Cheer up! I'm sure you and Mr. Winters will be invited to this year's ball," Mr. Toliver smiling said. "Yes, you're probably right," Nan replied but for the next question to Mr. Toliver she stopped drinking her tea to reluctantly ask… "Ooo…aah… Mr. Toliver?" "Yes," he turned to answer as he was walking out of the door. "Well, ah did aah Mrs. Utley receive an invitation, again this year?" "Why yes!

As a matter of fact she did. And oddly enough she asked me the same question about you just this morning," he said. "Oh, did she?" Nan responded smiling. "Yes, ma'am she did. And I personally hand delivered her ball invitation to her myself. You should have seen Mrs. Utley she was smiling as she was signing for it, made me feel real good too." Mr. Toliver replied. He was in a hurry "Oh, well Mrs. Winters I better get going I gotta finished delivering these ball invitations," But he stopped again to answer Nan's last questions. "Yes?" Mrs. Winters. "Well, Mr. Toliver I see you are extremely busy with your mail delivery and all but one last question, please," Nan requested, "Okay, Mrs. Winter, yes?" he replied. "Well, aum did ta'what about Mr. Utley did he received an invitation, as of yet?" Nan inquired. "No! Not yet!" Mr. Toliver replied. Nan felt somewhat relieved. "But as I tell most of my friends be prepared. I wouldn't wait until the last minute rushing out buying or have a gown made in a rush if I were you. Remember your invitations could come tomorrow," he told Nan. "Why, even my wife went out and bought her gown two weeks ago, just in case. You never know, so why not be prepared," "You know Mr. Toliver, you're right. I like that idea," she replied. As Mr. Toliver was leaving he thanked Nan again for the tea, stopping one more time to make a comment. "And speaking of my wife Mrs. Winters when I get home I'm going to have her make me another hot cup of tea, but this time I'll have her add something to it making it a little stronger to quiet my cough." "Oh, please do... Mr. Toliver, we wouldn't want that cough to develop into something more serious." "Yes, ma'am you're right! Mrs. Winters but I really must go. I'll see you tomorrow. Oh! I'll be, back later to pick-up my new fishing pole with my live bait. I can hardly wait to use them. Hey! By the way where's Alex I haven't seen him today?" he said. "Ah…he didn't come in today," Nan stated. "What? That's strange. That doesn't sound like Alex. Oh…well hope it's nothing serious," Mr. Toliver said, making inquiries. "No! I don't think so," Nan told him. "Well… tomorrow then." he said. "Yes, tomorrow," Nan sighed, ending her conversation with Mr. Toliver. Her mind and thoughts were still on Alex.

After the mailman left the shop Sturgis with Little Deek came in from working outside. "Yeah Nan, he's going to be a fine worker that Little Deek here," Sturgis spoke loud with enthusiasm. Later he pulled Nan close to him whispering," But you know dear, we have to see about getting that boy some real clothes. Clothes that actually fit him and it wouldn't hurt for him to learn how to match up his colors too," Then Sturgis resumed talking loud. Yeah… he's going to be a fine worker, that Little Deek." Nan tried to laugh but didn't. She was still worried about Alex. Sturgis could sense Nan's concern about Alex and he voiced his opinion, "Now, Nan darling don't worry about Alex. He's a young man now and is old enough to make his own decisions. He's also quite capable of taking care of himself and honestly dear he certainly doesn't need you mothering him all the time. And while we're on the subject of Alex let me add this to it. If I were you Nan, I wouldn't lose too much sleep over this whole thing, honestly," Nan was shocked she didn't want to believe that her husband could speak such uncompassionate words about Alex and wanting to comment on his remarks but Nan first had to take a seat to find, herself later saying, "How could you say that cold hearted remark about Alex?" she asked. "How, could I not say it, if it is true?" Sturgis quickly replied, then turned his focus back onto Little Deek, "See you in the morning Little Deek!" Sturgis said, smiling while waving bye to him.

"And now that we're still on the subject of Alex. Sturgis you could have shown more kindness towards him!" Nan shouted. "Oooh! I was waiting on that one, so now it's because of me as the reason why Alex is not here. Is that what you're implying, Nan?" Sturgis shouted. Nan didn't answer Sturgis right away she was quiet, stressed over Alex. And her long trip back home. She didn't know what to imply. "Oh! I don't know dear. I'm not thinking too clearly right about now, perhaps things will look better in the morning when Alex shows up," she said. "Well… I certainly hope so!" he sharply replied. Sturgis was rude and curt in his remarks to Nan, walking out of the room leaving her alone and still confused.

The night of the ball was fast approaching. Sturgis saw Mrs. Utley coming up the walk. With just Nan and he inside the shop Sturgis wanted to show a side of humor for a change. He needed to make up to Nan, get on her good side for making that cold remark about Alex nights ago. "Oh look dear! There comes Mrs. Utley. You can keep your seat, dear. I'll wait on this squawking, doubled-tongued, babbling, heifer. I'm sure she's here to brag about her invitation to the Governor's Ball," laughing he said. "Sturgis, dear please don't say that!" Nan said, laughing, seated, behind the counter. They both were still laughing when Mrs. Utley entered the gift shop. "And, may I asks, what's so funny?" She said entering, standing at the counter. "Did I miss a good tummy tickler? Or maybe that funny joke flew right out of the door when I opened it perhaps right over my head, too? Oh, come on now let me in on it," she said. Waiting for a reply, letting minutes passed, then adding, "Come on now. I'm still waiting I'd love to laugh right along with you two if I can. Let me hear it, too," Mrs. Utley stood facing the both of them tapping her foot on the wooden shop floor, in her restlessness of anticipation she still waited for a response. Neither Nan nor Sturgis had anything to say in their defense. "Ha! Just what I thought using the wisdom of silence, a good choice. Well, anyway, like I always say. If you can't speak the same words you just spoke in front of an interring, individual maybe, you ought not to speak them at all. Please, remember that!" The shop was silent with Mrs. Utley standing looking at the both of them Nan and Sturgis was hoping someone else would hurry and enter. But no one did. Then Mrs. Utley said. "Well, despite of what was said or what wasn't. Mrs. Winters and Mr. Winters I'm sure you both will agree and I must honestly announce this afternoon is beautiful! Wouldn't you say? "Yes, you are right. I totally agree," Sturgis said. Agreeing with Mrs. Utley, he needed to get in her good favor for laughing when she entered the shop. "And just think," Mrs. Utley taking in a deep breath continued to say, "You know. I ordered this day just for me!" smiling she said. "Yes, indeed. I must concur again it is a bright colorful afternoon." said, Sturgis, trying to sound serious in his reply. Then Mrs. Utley wanted to know how Tessa, Trent and the twins were. Nan told her when she left everyone was doing well. They were all happy about their surprise babies. "I bet they were, that was good news to hear," Mrs. Utley expressed further saying. "Now, I'm ready to use my trade credit. Oh, and just in case you haven't heard. I was one of the first, if not the first, to receive their invitation to the ball," she said, beaming with proudness, "Oh, really," Nan commented. "How wonderful for you Mrs. Utley, I know that made your day even better," Nan stated. "Yes, it did. But it only enhanced it. And you do know it's in two weeks, the ball I mean?" Mrs. Utley reminded them. "Yes, we know," Nan said. "Ahh, have either of you received your invitations, yet?" she asked. "We're still waiting," Nan replied. "Well, like I always say. Don't wait too long or this year's ball. Will have come and gone again and you will have missed going to this one too," Mrs. Utley laughing, said. Nan became a little annoyed, bothered by Mrs. Utley's comments. She had to quietly take in a deep breath to relax her nerves. But Sturgis was eager to wait on Mrs. Utley asking her, "Now, Mrs.

Utley on what item or items would you like to use your trade credit on?" smiling he asked. "Oh, how about a jeweled comb for my hair?" she replied, further saying, "My ball ensemble, is couture, only couture, you know. Now, I need something that glitters to wear in my hair?" Sturgis was standing at the counter he pulled the sparkling combs out placing them in front of her on the counter. "My…they are all so beautiful I don't know which one to choose!" she remarked. "How many would you like to buy? Why don't you all of them? " Smiling, he stated. "I think one should be enough. Oh, my goodness, are all these combs really from the sea?" she inquired. "Yes, ma'am from right out there," Nan said pointing toward the ocean. "They arrived in a shipwreck cargo from a long time ago they floated ashore in a wooden barrel along with other items about a year ago," Nan added, "How adventurous! What provenance! They could be queen's jewels," Mrs. Utley stated. "They could be," Nan replied. "Oh, my, imagine me wearing jewels that once belong to a queen, me, royalty. In that case give me a complete comb set with diamonds, rubies, emeralds, sapphires and those other loose sparkling gemstones. Oh, and da' I'll take all the black pearls, too," smiling she said.

But after looking at them a little closer, Mrs. Utley abruptly said, "Wait a minute! Aren't those jewels rather small for the price you're asking?" Mrs. Utley asked. Collecting his words with care, Sturgis answered. "Why, yes. One would think so but one would also see that they have eye catching luster with brilliances, wouldn't you say, Mrs. Utley?" He showing them to her again but this time, moving the jewels back n' forth to make them sparkle even more. "Well…Umm, I don't know?" She said, becoming reluctant to make the purchase. She was just about to change her mind. Sturgis could sense her backing out. So he quickly responded by adding these choice words to keep Mrs. Utley interest in buying the jewel. He invited Nan into his sales pitch. "You, know Nan dear, these jewels remind me of an extraordinary woman I must honestly say. A woman with superior class and sophistication," When Sturgis said those words he got Mrs. Utley's full attention. "They do? How is that dear?" Nan asked. Mrs. Utley stood at the counter looking up at Sturgis with her mouth almost opened listening attentively. Not only was she taken in by his handsomeness but by every word he spoke as he described to her the perfect woman. In Mrs. Utley mind Sturgis was talking about her. Mrs. Utley's pride puffed up even more as he voiced, inflating her haughtiness and vain ego. She stood facing him, looking at his gorgeous face, as he described the ideal woman. "Why, yes let me expound, further, may I please?" he asked. "Please do," Mrs. Utley intervened. "Yes, you see. A woman that wears these exquisite jeweled combs in her hair would be sending a strong message to every woman that sees her. That she is a woman with influence, wealth and prestige. To be quite frank with you dear, she would be a cut above every woman on this earth. And in the eyes of a man, that kind of woman would always demand his full attention. Showing him that she has class with style, along with sophistication, of course," Sturgis said. As he watched Mrs. Utley bite the bait, "And Nan dear, what woman wouldn't want to own, love. Even wear, these beautiful jeweled combs in her hair. Especially, at this year's Governor's Ball. Why, she would be the only woman making the only true fashion statement of wealth and power," Sturgis couldn't finish speaking those words fast enough, when Mrs. Utley quickly expressed, "Oh, wait! How true! You're right! Look no further! That's me you just described. I'm that kind of woman. That woman is me," Mrs. Utley, said almost shouting, from excitement, further stating. "And, said Mr. Winters, I'm that only woman! Wrap em' up! I'll take em' and put the balance owed on my husband's account, would you please." Mrs. Utley was happy with her new order. She gladly hurried in demanding Nan to carry out her request to complete the jewels she had purchased, "After, Sturgis finished speaking with Mrs. Utley, he turned to winked at Nan, almost laughing out loud. When in walked Mr. Lowell, "Well, hello Mr. Lowell," Mrs. Utley said, acknowledging him. "Mrs. Utley," Warren replied. "Well, now. Mr. Warren, tell me have you or Ms. La' Cure received your invitations to the ball, yet?" She asked. Sturgis gave Nan the combs to wrap for Mrs. Utley. "Yes, Mrs. Utley! As a matter of fact we have," Warren said, looking at Sturgis with great suspicion and distrust. "Marvelous! Well then…I know you and your lovely Ya'vett will be the highlight of the evening," Mrs. Utley stated, later telling him she had to run but would see them at the ball.

Nan finished wrapping the package she handed it to Mrs. Utley. They both walked to her carriage talking about Tessa's new twin babies. "I was under the impression that Ms. La' Cure was coming here today to pick up her paintings. I had something else I thought she'd might be interested in seeing," Sturgis said. "Not this time Winters!" Warren cleverly replied. "And so that you'll know Ms. La' Cure has already shared with me about your, shall we say art viewing tactics? And as you well know, she and I are engaged to be married soon. So, I thought I may as well get use to running some of her or my wife's errands. Especially in places where, I think one individual is of unsavory character." Sturgis kept silent standing behind the counter as Warren talked about Ya'vett. He too was thinking about her only softly, smiling, running his tongue across his lower lip. Then he reached down putting back the black felt jewelry trays Nan left out on the counter, wishing it was his lovely Ya'vett he was holding in his hands instead. What Warren has come to realize is that Sturgis has everything a woman needs in a man; masculinity, courage, conversation and looks but no money? Warren on the other hand, has wealth, influence, lots of money to afford Ya'vett or any woman who enters his life. But lacks everything Sturgis Winters possesses as a man. When Warren finished talking Sturgis opened the delivery book to write down information told to him by Warren. "Ms. La' Cure would like them, delivered next Wednesday, at 2pm," "That will be perfect," Sturgis said. "And please inform, Ms. La.

Cure I shall be prompt with her delivery. She can expect me at 2pm,"
"No! Winters. We'll both be expecting you," Warren rudely responded.
Sturgis just smiled knowing he had annoyed Warren as he wrote down
the information. Then he closed the book, looking Warren straight in the
eyes saying. "You don't care that much for me, do you Warren?" Sturgis
asked. "No! Not particularly," Warren responded. "Why?" Sturgis asked.
"Because you're vile, vulgar and everything about you wreaks
rottenness. You're no good Winters." Warren was adamant in his say to
Sturgis. "Ooh, really," He chucked once surprised at Warren answer,
commenting. "Oh, well that's just your opinion. And it's not a fair
assessment of me. Sturgis said, then looked at Warren with a serious
look on his face, saying. "I'll tell you what, Warren let's get a second
opinion...why don't you ask Ms. La' Cure how good I am," he said, with
a grin on his face. "Furthermore, Warren, please inform Ms. La' Cure I
am always willing, available, with readiness to fulfill any request or
desire she may have now or in the future." Hearing that from Sturgis,
Warren had no comment. He was angered, storming out of the gift shop
in a rage, rushing by Nan and Mrs. Utley without speaking to either of
them or saying good-bye. They watched with concern as his carriage
sped away.

Moments after Warren and Mrs. Utley left, the shop. It began to fill with
excited, chattering men and women, buying to look their best for a one
night of the year extravaganza. "The Ball"…snobbishness went with
discussion on color, style of gowns or tuxedos. Attitudes were worn on
shoulders of those who received an invitation. While those that hadn't
received an invitation shopped in silence. Keeping quiet with hopes of
getting there's in the mail. It was obvious inside the gift shop, that
everyone going felt they had bragging rights. With two weeks left…
"Dear, it looks as though I won't be going again this year to the ball,
either," Nan said with sadness. "Now, Nan dear, be optimistic. We have
two weeks left and if we don't go this year it isn't the end of the world.
Now is it?" he said. Nan slowly spoke, "I guess you're right Sturgis.
And dear, if you don't mind as soon as a few more shoppers leave I
think I'll go into one of the inventory rooms to work in there for a while..
If you need my help, just buzz will you dear," Nan said. "That will be
fine Nan and it might even do you some good to be alone back there
away from shoppers up here with their constant chattering and, talking
about the ball. Making my wife feel sad all over again," he empathized
with her, kissing Nan on the cheek to help make her feel better. Sturgis
waited on the last customer from the shopping rush. He was about to
take his seat behind the counter to rest when a fill-in postman for Mr.
Toliver working his route arrived. "Where's Mr. Toliver?" Sturgis asked.
"Oh, he's out sick today, maybe all this week, too," He replied. "Oh!
Sorry to hear that news. Give him our best," "Will, do sir," "Wait, don't
leave yet, this isn't our mail!" Sturgis said. Flipping through a bundle of
shop mail handed him by the mailman. "Oh, sorry I've been doing that
all day. This is the first time I've worked this route I'm not use to the

names, yet," the postman replied. "Well, that's obvious," Sturgis remarked handing back to the mailman all misdelivered mail he delivered in error to the gift shop. "It will take some time for you to familiarize yourself with names and faces around here but it's doable," Sturgis remarked. "Wait! This isn't ours either. Oh here you can drop this piece of mail off three shops down from us at Friedman's," Sturgis added. "Why, thank you, sir. See you tomorrow," the postman said. "Yeah, thanks," grumpy Sturgis replied. He was still seated behind the counter flipping through the mail. When suddenly he stopped with a look of joy and jubilation on his face as he gazed down at the mail he was holding in his hands. "Ooh, Nan, dear come quick!" Sturgis shouted with excitement!

He was holding two invitations for the ball in his hands. And not able to wait for Nan to come into the room he eagerly opened one to read...*Mrs. Sturgis Winters, You are cordially invited with Platinum Status to attend The Annual 24 Hr., Governor's Ball to be held at the Governor's Mansion on...* "Be there in a minute, dear," Nan shouted. Sturgis was still smiling. He was waiting for Nan to come into the room. In his wait, he looked down at the next piece of mail he was holding in his hands. He saw it was delivered to the gift shop in error. It was a letter for Ms. La' Cure and seeing her name of the envelope made his heart almost stopped. "Ms. Ya'vett La' Cure," Sturgis whispered. He thought of her with deep desires that made his mouth begin to water. *"Ms. La' Cure... So love worthy."* He whispered, gently rubbing his fingers across her name on the envelope, as his heart raced with passions of imaginations for her. And he, not wanting that feeling to end, suddenly realized it wouldn't have to. "The Ball" would be the perfect place for him to fulfill his enchanting night of fantasy with her. Sturgis would have that one night. That one chance to make it all come, true. "Here, I come dear," Nan said. Sturgis thinking fast and quick grabbed at random a book from the bookshelf, he placed Nan's invitation inside a page and slammed the book closed. Then he put it back on the shelf amongst the other books. He hurried and stuffed his invitation with Ms. La' Cure's letter inside his work vest pocket and... "Yes dear what is it? What's so important? You sound so excited. I thought you might have heard word about Alex," Nan said coming into the room, "Who me? No! Oh, did I sound like it was important? Um, I'm sorry if I did. It was nothing. I just needed some numbers to something but I figured it out. See..." he said, showing Nan a wrinkled piece of paper he got out of his wallet with old numbers on it. "See dear this is all. See, I told you it was nothing, nothing at all dear." answering Nan with a nervous tone in his voice, after hiding her invitation in a rush.

"I, see the mail is in?" said Nan. "Oh, is it? Yeah, ah that's right I forgot," Sturgis answered. "Look Sturgis, dear an invitation to the ball!" Nan said with excitement holding the invitation in her hand. Sturgis' heart raced with fear. He was thinking in his haste he'd accidentally dropped Nan's invitation on the floor near the counter. "An invitation…an invitation to what dear!" he almost shouted with readiness conjuring up an excuse to tell her. Opening his mouth to speak… "Now, Nan…" he started to say. "Oh, how wonderful they didn't forget!" Nan said cutting his words off. "Now, Listen Nan…" he tried saying using his hands to express himself. In her excitement she overtook the conversation from Sturgis, "Nan as I was…"he said but she cut his words off again. So Sturgis decided to wait and see who his wife was actually talking about. He was waiting for her to finish expressing her excitement about the invitation. And in his wait to him she was taking too long to say the name of the person on the invitation she was holding. With apprehension and anticipation Sturgis was beginning to squirm in his chair. He wanted to know who Nan was making reference to. Unable to wait any longer…he cut her words off. Right in the middle of her sentence, shouting, "Forget who? Who did they not forget, Nan?" he almost shouted at her and was hoping she wasn't talking about herself. "Oh, I'm so sorry dear," Nan almost laughing with joy said. "It's the great lady of the theatre Sturgis! That's who I'm talking about, this invitation, is for. The great and famous Ms. Shel'Leese Verlon, dear, that's what I've been trying to tell you." "Oooh," with a sigh of relief, he happily said. "Oh, Yeah, I've heard of her," Sturgis stated, sitting back down in his chair, he shook the wrinkles out of the newspaper, crossed his legs at the ankles and resumed reading, becoming comfortable again. Later, he took in a deep breath letting it out, relaxing, and regaining his comfort. While commenting, "She's rather up in age now isn't she, dear?" he asked and he was glad Nan wasn't talking about herself. "Yes, she is but after all these years… Ms. Verlon finally receives the invitation she so badly deserved. I'm glad for her, even though she may never know about this invitation. She will always be the lady of the theatre to me," Nan replied. "Well, dear from what I've heard about her great performances I have to agree with you and all her fans around the world. She will always be that starlet of the stage," Sturgis said as he placed his newspaper on the table. Then he got up from Nan's rocking chair stretched and went into the next room. He was thinking of a way to let Nan know his invitation came in the mail, without raising suspicions about hers. And he had only a short time in which to do it.

A week had gone by. Sturgis was hoping Mr. Toliver was still out sick. *"The fill-in mailman, he'll be perfect,"* Sturgis whispered to himself. But first he needed to see which mailman was coming to deliver mail today. So Sturgis put his invitation back inside the work vest pocket he was wearing. And waited on the mailman to arrive hoping it wasn't Mr. Toliver. And seconds later, it wasn't. "Good afternoon sir. Here's your mail," he said. Sturgis not wanting to encourage a lengthy conversation with the mailman he, invented a scheme. To give the impression that he was repairing a very valuable pocket watch. So when the mailman entered the shop. He wouldn't have to carry on a long conversation with him that might cause Nan to come up front into the shop asking about her invitation. The mailman entered the shop. Sturgis sat at the counter wearing an eyeglass piece on his left eye, having the back of a watch opened, exposed, with little tools next to it, faking the whole watch repairing process. "Oh, is that you postman? Thank you," Sturgis replied, in a low curt tone so Nan wouldn't hear him. "As you can see, I can't talk now. I'm very busy repairing a very old, rare and expensive pocket watch. This is a very delicate, complexed, procedure sorry I can't talk now. Place the mail on the counter. See you tomorrow," Sturgis said never once raising his head to look at the man. He kept looking down giving the illusion he was busy repairing the fine intricate pieces of a rare valuable pocket watch. "Alright sir," the postman was quick to say. "I wouldn't want you to stop and talk to me messing up that delicate procedure. I'm placing your mail on the counter as you instructed." He did. Then, the mailman left the shop. Sturgis waited until the shop door closed. He threw the eyepiece down on the counter stood to his feet rushed to the window to make sure the postman was completely out of view. Then Sturgis reached for the invitation inside his vest pocket mixing it in with today's mail, he waited a few seconds took in a deep breath and shouted, "Oh…Nan dear, look it came! It came! It finally came! My invitation to the ball is here! "Your what?" Nan shouted back then rushed into the shop from the inventory room. "What dear? What did you say? What came?" she said. "See dear… it came. The invitation it came just now!" Sturgis said. "Let me see that Sturgis!" Nan said she was elated, "Oh my! You're right!" she said with her hands were shaking from excitement. Nan could barely contain herself. She quickly removed the waxed seal reading his invitation out loud. Then waited a few minutes to calm down, after collecting her composure Nan said, "Oh…Sturgis I am so happy for you. I know you're excited too, dear," she told him giving him a kiss and a hug, "How nice! How wonderful for you, dear. After a few minutes Nan settled down she was almost out of breath from the excitement. Then she asked. Now, dear did mine come?" She was still a little excited but wanted to know if her invitation came. "Yours…?" Sturgis was careful he was clever with his answer to Nan. "Well… I don't know dear to be honest with you I didn't check today's mail for yours I was so excited when I saw mine. I forgot to look for yours, right then but I'm sure it's here dear…Let's take a look see," he told her smiling. Sturgis looked through the mail again, pretending to be looking for Nan's invitation. Finally he said, "No! Dear I'm afraid I don't see yours here…hum." Then he handed Nan the stack of mail, telling her to look through it again. Saying, he must have overlooked it in all the excitement. Nan eagerly looked through the mail, "No! Dear it's not here," she answered. "Hmmm…" Sturgis sighed further, saying. "Now, that is strange. How can that be?" He remarked pretending to be looking around the counter floor area for Nan's invitation, "Maybe it dropped somewhere around here. Let me see. Let me look over here, dear," Later, asking Nan. "Do you see anything on the floor over there near you Nan, dearest?" he asked with sincerity. Nan looked around on the shop floor for her invitation, "No … I don't see anything on the floor over here, either," she answered. "Hmm…Now that's odd," he replied scratching his head trying to look confused. "Are you sure this is all the mail?" Nan was upset but inquired. "Yes…dear that's all the mail for today," Sturgis replied. "Now, that's odd, strange wouldn't you say Sturgis," Nan commented, "What do you mean, dear?" he asked. "Well, now, you got your invitation but mine didn't come. I would say that is rather odd. Wouldn't you?" Nan commented. "Now, Nan dear, don't worry. It could still come tomorrow I'm sure it will come tomorrow," he responded, "Tomorrow!" She frantically replied. "Tomorrow is the day of the ball, Sturgis!" "Oooh, yeah, you're right Nan, Well?" he replied. Nan was slow, to intervened saying, "Oooh, maybe you're right. I don't know. It could still quite possibly come tomorrow, But I doubt if it comes tomorrow or at all," disgusted she said. Then Sturgis commented, "Well, dear, I wouldn't be too hard on myself if I were you? One never knows about these things. We will just have to wait to see what tomorrow will bring us, now won't we, Nan?" he said kissing her on the forehead. "Oh, I guess so," Nan unhappily replied going into the kitchen to pour her a cup of hot tea.

She didn't sleep well that night. And to her it seemed the sun was up extra early the next day. Nan slept late. It was the day of the ball, she was melancholy all day. Only one customer came in to shop it was a man who purchased a silk scarf for his wife to wear tonight at the ball. Those that received an invitation were busy at home preparing for tonight's big event. Those that didn't stayed away for fear of embarrassment. Nan was unhappy because it seemed that everyone, including her husband, received an invitation. "Well…Sturgis it looks as though I won't be going to the ball again this year," she said flipping through the mail again, one letter at a time. Then putting it on the counter, Nan sighed, "Sturgis, are you sure this is all the mail for today?" she asked. "That's all the mail, Nan dear, he replied. Thinking quickly to appease her, he said, "How dare they not invite you, my wife, to their ol' stuffy, stiff necked ball? Why, I'm still so upset they didn't invite you dear. "I have a good mind not to go, myself!" he stated later, picking her up by the waist, watching Nan's reactions. He then gently placed her down hugging, kissing her trying to console his wife. "Don't be ridiculous," Nan almost smiling replied. "You will go Sturgis! And you will represent Mr. and Mrs. Sturgis Winters' with the highest respect, good taste, along with an excellent style for fashion. I won't have it any other way, do you hear me!" Nan was strong in her request to her husband. Sturgis was content with his wife's remarks. He felt he had won…"Yes, dear if that will make you happy, then I'll go," he said. "That will make me happy Sturgis," she replied. That evening Nan helped Sturgis dress for the Governor's Ball an annual gala event. Finally it was time for the last, finishing touches…his accent accessories: gold cufflinks, gold watch and a platinum bracelet. Lastly she straightened his black stain bowtie. Then Nan stood back smiling, looking at her handsome husband dressed in his black fitted tuxedo with all the accessories. She took in a deep breath commenting, "…Oh, my goodness Sturgis, if Narcissus was invited to this ball, he would have to leave, when you entered the room." Even Sturgis had to blush upon hearing Nan's compliments about him as he stood looking at himself in the mirror, voicing. "Why, thank you dear. And what I'm about to say. I say with great humility, *Yes dear you are right. Narcissus would have to leave.*" But I still hate to leave you here all alone. I won't go!" He said toying with Nan. "Now, Sturgis Winters don't be childish, I'll be fine. I'll just have a cup of hot milk and sit by the fireplace soon I'll drift off to sleep. And when you come home you can tell me all about the ball," Nan said walking her husband arm and arm to the door. Then she watched him board his carriage dressed in the highest of fashion, waving good-bye. She couldn't help but feel sad, "Be home before tomorrow's dawn," she shouted. "Be home before tomorrow's dawn," squawked Asza. Nan quickly covered his cage for the night. She tried to relax by the fireplace, sitting in her wooden rocker, sipping her cup of hot milk with E-la the cat curled at her feet.

But she was too fidgety, still upset because she was not invited to the ball. So she decided to get up and move around, going over near the bookshelf to look at Ms. Verlon's ball invitation again. Yawning…Nan placed her cup of hot milk on the counter as she read Ms. Verlon's invitation in silence, smiling, not really sleepy.

She reached for a book on the bookshelf running her index finger across book binders stopping on one. Yawning, again then skimming through the pages looking for a book with pictures. Flipping through the pages of the book, her invitation to the ball dropped to the floor.

She looked down and saw her name on a white parchment envelope. *"For Mrs. Sturgis Winters,"* she picked it up, opened it and read, *"Respectfully for Mrs. Sturgis Winters with Platinum Status you are cordially…"*

TO BE CONTINUED…

www.ingramcontent.com/pod-product-compliance
Lightning Source LLC
Chambersburg PA
CBHW070224140626
46555CB00018B/1271